the cannibals

Cynthia D. Grant

speak
An Imprint of Penguin Group (USA) Inc.

SPEAK

Published by Penguin Group

Penguin Group (USA) Inc.,

345 Hudson Street, New York, New York 10014, U.S.A.

Penguin Books Ltd, 80 Strand, London WC2R ORL, England

Penguin Books Australia Ltd, 250 Camberwell Road,

Camberwell, Victoria 3124, Australia

Penguin Books Canada Ltd, 10 Alcorn Avenue, Toronto, Ontario, Canada M4V 3B2

Penguin Books (N.Z.) Ltd, 182-190 Wairau Road, Auckland 10, New Zealand

First published in the United States of America under the title
The Cannibals: Starring Tiffany Spratt by Roaring Brook Press,
a division of The Millbrook Press, Inc., 2002

Published by Speak, an imprint of Penguin Group (USA) Inc., 2004

3 5 7 9 10 8 6 4 2

Speak ISBN 0-14-240127-7

Printed in the United States of America

the cannibals

Chapter One

The most incredibly fantastic thing happened at school today. It's enough to make you believe in God. Which I already do, of course. Just kidding, God!

The best-looking boy I've ever seen has transferred to Hiram Johnson High!

I ran into him in the parking lot this morning. You should see his car. It's a green Mercedes. I think it's a Mercedes. It might be a Honda. Actually you *have* seen his car because you're me and I'm you and what is the point of keeping this journal? Miss Jones says it will teach us to be more observant and put us in touch with our thoughts and feelings and help us learn to write concise sentences instead of just rambling on and on.

"Those are skills you need to work on, Tiffany," she said.

For *some* reason she thinks I'm in too much of a

hurry and don't pay enough attention to what's going on in the world around me, particularly in her class.

Miss Jones explained that she isn't going to read our journals, just glance through them to make sure we're actually writing something, otherwise we'll get an Incomplete and won't graduate in June and our lives will be ruined. Barbie's just writing "I am so bored" over and over, but I figure I might as well do something. Who knows: Maybe my grandkids will see this someday! What a horrible thought. If I ever get that old, I am *definitely* getting a face-lift, but by then scientists will probably have figured something out so that people don't die or at least won't get wrinkles.

But instead of writing my journal, I've decided to videotape it, which is a lot more creative than putting words on paper. Besides, when I write, my hand gets all crampy. The *last* thing I need is that carpal tunnel syndrome. Then how could I do cartwheels and hand-stands? Plus, videotaping myself gives me modeling practice and I can study the tapes and see how I'm sitting. It's *amazing* how many girls just *sprawl* at their desks, like they think they're invisible from the waist down.

I figure if I have to, I can always pay someone to put all these thoughts and feelings on paper. Miss Jones hasn't approved the video cam yet. She's such a dinosaur, but I guess you can't blame her—she spent most of her whole life in another century.

Anyway, the boy in the parking lot this morning was so *unbelievably handsome* I went over and said, "Hi! Are you a new student?" Duh, like he could be the new janitor or something.

"Yes," he said. "We just moved up from Los Angeles. I wanted to be here when school started, but the house wasn't ready."

He lives in that new development, I forget what it's called, Weasel Creek or something, with the gigantic houses on the teensy little lots—and it turns out *he's* a senior, too.

I can't believe how well this year is starting out!

"You haven't missed much," I said. "By the way, I'm Tiffany Spratt, Head Yell Leader at Hi High."

"Cannibal MacLaine." He shook my hand.

Cannibal! What an incredibly unusual name, but he *did* say he was from Los Angeles.

"Really," I said. "That's so cool."

"My mom's Scottish," he explained, whatever that meant, but I didn't have time to figure it out because right then I was having a major brain flash: THE CAN-NIBALS could be the name of our group! Why should everybody but me and The Girls have a gang? That's all you ever hear about on the news. Not that we want

3

to steal stuff or beat people up or get tattoos. We just think it would be fun to be a real group, with our own name and style and everything.

The Cannibals! Talk about an inspiration!

As I escorted Cannibal into the school, everybody was staring at us, not only because we looked so good together, but because I wasn't with Wally. Don't get me wrong—I still love Wally. But lately he's kind of getting on my nerves. He wants to be with me every second. No matter where I go, he has to be there, too. It's like—I don't want this to come out wrong—but it's like he's the gum and I'm the shoe.

Another reason Cannibal and I looked so great together was because I was wearing my blue sweater that matches my eyes—and his—and his hair is blond, like mine. Talk about a coincidence! Luckily, I shampooed this morning and my hair was sparkling clean. Some people think eyes are the windows of the soul, but personally, I think it's hair.

The last time she trimmed me, Marge said, "I want you to try this new shampoo, Tiffany. It'll make you fall in love with your hair. Remember, hair is like a fine fabric."

Finally, someone who takes hair seriously! My mother's threatened to cut mine off while I'm asleep, but I don't think she really means it.

4

As Cannibal and I walked down the hall to the attendance office, I was thinking about that TV show that's set in a high school and how they should make a show about *our* school. They could call it *Hi High* and it would be all about me and The Girls and our exciting adventures as cheerleaders, and Cannibal could play my boyfriend in the show, and Wally will just have to get used to it.

I wanted to wait and walk Cannibal to his room, but the secretary said, "Tiffany, you're late for class again."

"That's okay," I said. "It's just English."

Dean Schmitz came out of his office and squinted at me.

"Aren't you supposed to be somewhere?" he said.

So I had to go, but Cannibal said, "Thanks," and I could tell it was from the heart.

I couldn't *wait* to find The Girls and tell them about Cannibal and how we were going to call our group **The Cannibals**. Unfortunately, The Girls were already in class, but then I got this brilliant idea: We could get T-shirts or jackets with **The Cannibals** printed on them! It would look supercool and *everybody* would want to be a **Cannibal**, but we'd have to say "sorry," but be really nice about it so we wouldn't hurt anybody's feelings.

I drove to the mall but it was still closed, so I went

to the gas station and drank low-fat mochas until the stores opened at ten.

Then I went to the Quik Print shop where they personalize T-shirts and hats, et cetera. I thought about making some bumper stickers, too, but then I thought, no sense going overboard, we can always do that later.

I told the girl behind the counter that I wanted five red sweatshirts and five red T-shirts: one for me, Shelby, Barbie, Kendall, and Ashley, with our names printed on the back and **The Cannibals** on the front in big black letters.

"The *what*?" the girl said.

"**The Cannibals**." I wrote it down, just in case. She didn't exactly look like the world's best speller.

"How are you gonna pay for this?" she demanded.

I showed her my mother's Visa card, which I borrowed last week and forgot to give back.

"You're Elizabeth Spratt?"

"Yes," I said. There wasn't time to go into all that. "And I need the shirts today."

"Today?"

"It's kind of an emergency," I explained.

The girl's eyeballs rolled up like she was having a mini-seizure but she said, "Okay, come back later."

I did some shopping while I waited and it was great. The mall isn't crowded at all on school days! I got a really cute blouse and some shoes and a jacket.

Then I bought some earrings and a couple of posters and an ice cream cone, mint chip and jamoca almond fudge, and when I went back to the Quik Print place, the shirts were ready.

They looked *great*! I couldn't wait for The Girls to see them! School was almost over, so I asked the girl if I could use the phone. You'd have thought I wanted to borrow her *toothbrush*, but finally she handed it over. Luckily, the school can't afford videophones, or things might not have gone so smoothly.

I called the attendance office and said, "This is Mrs. Ramirez. May I speak to Shelby, please?"

The secretary wanted me to leave a message, but I said no, it was too personal.

Shelby *finally* came to the phone—the girl was giving me looks like I was phoning Hong Kong—and I said, "Hello, darling. Did you remember to wipe?" and Shelby said, "Mother, is that you?"

I told her about Cannibal and how handsome he is, and she said, "I know. I couldn't agree with you more, Mother."

Then I told her how he gave me this *fabulous* idea for the name of our group and she thought it was fabulous, too, and said she'd get The Girls and they'd meet me in the parking lot after school.

They were waiting when I got there: Shelby, Ashley, and one of the twins—I thought it was Kendall but it turned out to be Barbie; Kendall was practicing her synchronized swimming—and I showed them the shirts and they were like, omigod! It's like we're in a *rock group* or something!

"I know!" I said. "That's exactly what I was thinking!"

So then we started thinking we could be a *real* band. Ashley has a great voice and Kendall plays the piano, and Shelby used to play the saxophone until she saw a picture of how it makes her face look.

Barbie said, "Everybody's going to want to be in our group!"

But they can't, because we've been friends forever, practically since kindergarten, and also because most people aren't as good-looking as us, and it would make them feel insecure. I know that sounds conceited, but it's true.

The Girls formed a screen around me so I could put on my new T-shirt; then Shelby said, "Isn't that Cannibal coming?"

I ran over to his car and said, "Hi, remember me?"

"Of course," he said, smiling. His teeth are so white they could be in a gum commercial!

"How was school today?" I asked.

"Just fine," he answered. "People here are really nice."

"I have a surprise for you," I told him. "Look!"

I guess he thought I was pointing at my breasts. He looked confused.

"No," I said, "the T-shirt! The *name*."

"Wow," he said. "That's cool. Are you in some kind of group or something?"

"Yes." I pointed at The Girls. They waved. "But it's also kind of in honor of you."

"Me?" he said.

"Well, yeah, because you're new at school and because it's such a cool name. It's the most unusual name I've ever heard."

"What do you mean?" he persisted.

Was this guy in Special Ed or *what*? How could anyone that handsome be so dumb?

"That's your name, isn't it?"

"What's my name?"

"Cannibal!"

"No," he said. "It's Campbell. Campbell MacLaine. It's Scottish."

"Oh," I said.

But we've decided to keep the name for our group since we've already got the shirts.

Chapter Two

Something intensely *strange* happened in computer class today.

Mr. Brewer was telling his teenagers joke again—"One; he holds the lightbulb in place and expects the whole world to revolve around him, har har"—when suddenly the door's *kicked* open and twelve guys in black suits and really cool sunglasses rush in and throw Mr. Brewer on the floor, shouting, "Everybody stay where you are! Don't move!"

As if we would! It was better than an episode of *Dead Crooks*, starring all of us, especially Mr. Brewer.

At first I thought the men were terrorists who'd hold us hostage while the whole country watched us on TV and prayed. But it turns out they were the FBI and that someone's been using the school's Internet hookup to hack into the Pentagon's computers!

Then Principal Brown and Dean Schmitz ran in,

and everybody yelled at everybody else, and it was real exciting and confusing.

The agents demanded to see what was on our computer screens, and Mr. Brewer cried, "For heaven's sake, they're researching college campuses!"

Which wasn't exactly true. At that moment I was checking out a psychic in LA that I'd heard about on an infomercial.

A few girls were crying and the boys looked scared, but like I kept saying, "We've got nothing to hide!" Besides, nothing terrible had happened. Apparently, a few bombers got mistakenly sent to some tiny little island, but nobody even lives there!

The FBI guys started hauling the computers and wastebaskets out of the room and Principal Brown left to call the school attorney. Meanwhile, a bunch of news guys had materialized outside the windows and were taking pictures until the FBI guys pulled down the shades. Drat.

They questioned each of us students—talk about *rude*. I didn't think the FBI would act like that! Then we finally got to leave. I made a quick stop in the john to check my hair. It was holding up beautifully.

The halls were jammed and people were *totally* freaking out. Mrs. Martin's whole class was crouched under their desks! They thought there'd been an earthquake or a bomb threat or something.

Outside, the reporters were interviewing the kids standing around, which really ticked me off. None of those kids was even in the room when it happened! Luckily, I spotted Marcy Richmond, the Channel 7 News gal. I explained that I was the school's Head Yell Leader and had been trapped in the raided classroom with the FBI, so if *anybody* knew what was happening, it was me.

Marcy signaled to her cameraman and he started filming. Then she said, "We're here at Hiram Johnson High School, where FBI agents have determined that the school's Internet system has been used to breach national security . . . *blah-blah-blah* . . . with a student who was trapped in the raided classroom. Your name, young lady?"

I wondered. Was this the right moment to drop the "Spratt," which sounds so, I don't know, flat and boring, and just be known by my first name alone, which is what I've always planned to do professionally?

"Tiffany Spratt," I decided, looking right into the camera. "Head Yell Leader at Hiram Johnson High."

"Tiffany, can you describe what you witnessed in the classroom?"

"I'd be glad to, Marcy," I began. "What started out like any other day was suddenly—" But at that moment, Dean Schmitz *lifted me up* and set me down somewhere else.

"Thank you, Miss Spratt, that will be all," he said, and then he was hogging the camera.

It was maddening.

Principal Brown was going around telling everybody to go back to class, but I drove home and put on my **Cannibals** sweatshirt and set the VCR to tape the five o'clock news.

My father came out of the room he uses as his office and said, "Tiffany, why does it say **The Cannibals** on your sweatshirt?"

There wasn't time to go into all that. "It's the name of our school mascot, Daddy."

Actually, the dolphin is our official school mascot, but all the other schools laugh at our teams and call us the Fighting Fish. Could we possibly *change* our mascot to **The Cannibals**?

"That's rather odd, isn't it?" he queried.

"I have to run, Daddy. Talk to you later," I said.

When I got back to school, the campus was an absolute madhouse, but I finally found Marcy and her cameraman. She asked me what **The Cannibals** meant and I explained that we were thinking about changing our school mascot. Then she said, "Tell me, Tiffany, how do you feel about Mr. Brewer?"

I explained that I was practically positive that Mr. Brewer wasn't a spy, and that he would *never* approve of any of his students horsing around with the Defense Department.

I knew he'd appreciate that.

Finally, the reporters and the FBI left and rumors were flying around campus. Like, whoever broke into the Pentagon—and I heard a million guesses—would probably go to prison and be on television and get offered a big job with Microsoft. Kendall even heard that the president (of our country) was flying out to personally thank the *perpetrators* for pointing out this potentially fatal flaw in our national security.

Come to think of it, *Wally* said something about the Pentagon the other night, but I thought he was talking about one of his stupid video games. Sometimes I think he loves them more than me!

At dinner tonight my parents were all worked up about the FBI raid: "What if somebody had gotten hurt?" et cetera, et cetera. But the only person who almost got hurt was my *brother*, who'd somehow messed up the

VCR and accidentally taped an old episode of *Quincy*, so I never got to see myself on the news!

"It's not like I did it on purpose!" he whined. Which is probably true; he's only a freshman.

"Were you scared, Tiff?" asked my father.

"Of what?" I plucked a piece of salad off my mother's plate. She tried to stab my fingers with her fork.

"Do you mind, Tiffany?"

She's so touchy lately. I think it must be the Change of Life, some kind of hormonal deal. The other day I was telling her how much younger she'd look if she'd just get her jowls tucked—we're not talking a major overhaul here—and she grabbed me and said, "Who *are* you? What have you done with my little girl?"

"By the way," I announced, "from now on I'm going to drop the 'Spratt' and just use my first name professionally."

Dad said, "What do you mean, 'professionally,' Tiff?"

"You know, in my modeling and acting career."

"Like Mr. Ed!" my brother snorted, referring to this *horse* on an ancient TV show.

"I had a hairdresser named Mr. Ed," my mother said. "Tiffany, did you finish those college applications?"

"Not yet," I said. I've had so much on my mind: Campbell, and **The Cannibals**, and Wally—I have *got* to return his call—not to mention my job at Macy's, where I model teen fashions in their shows and newspaper ads.

"You'd better get those applications done," she said. "You can't be a teenager forever, Tiffany. It's not a career option."

"I realize that, Mother." How dense does she think I am? "That's where my modeling career comes in."

"Which is fine for now," my father said, "but not something you'll want to do indefinitely."

"No," I said. "I also plan to be a famous actress. I truly believe that when God gives you these gifts, you have a sacred duty to use them."

"Which gifts are you referring to, Tiff?" my mother asked.

"Well, without sounding conceited about it," I said, "I'm pretty beautiful."

"Oh, brother!" my brother snickered.

"Beauty is not a talent," my father said, smiling. "It's something that happens accidentally."

No kidding. Not that my parents aren't cute in their own way. Don't get me wrong, I love them a lot, but lately it seems like we're from different planets. I mean, I realize that teaching second grade isn't a glam-

16

orous job, but couldn't my mother at *least* wear some makeup? She doesn't even shave her underarms.

"Any nut can be famous these days," my mother said. "The important thing now is to get a good education so that you can do something worthwhile with your life."

And so forth. And it's true what she said: In the old days you had to actually *do* something to be famous, like win the Olympics, or a war, or write a book. But now you can get famous just by being really *weird*, like those kids in Nebraska who ate their parents. "How *could* they?" Shelby shuddered when we heard the news. "I don't even like to *kiss* my parents!"

My father said, "Do you understand what we're trying to tell you, honey?"

"Of course I do, Daddy," I said. "What's for dessert?"

One thing really lucky about me: I can eat whatever I want and not gain weight. My mother says I have the metabolism of a mosquito.

After dessert, my father went into his office to take some calls. He used to own an advertising agency, but now he works at home. He's what they call an "idea man." I'm very proud of all that he's accomplished.

It was my father who came up with the concept for the *Television Land* subdivisions now sweeping the country, with homes designed exactly like the ones in old shows: the Brady, the Nelson, the Huxtable, the Cleaver.

His latest concept has *really* taken off: full-service gas stations, where you don't have to put in the gas yourself. People in uniforms come out and do it and even check your oil and wash your windshield!

But I'm worried about him lately. He hasn't been the same since Gramma died, two years ago. "Nobody loves us as much as our own mothers," he'd sigh. "Nobody else ever finds us so fascinating."

That's how he got the idea for 1-800-YOR-MAMA, a free public service for people who miss their moms. He hired a bunch of nice old ladies, and people call them up and tell them all their problems. The old ladies make little clucking sounds and say, "That's terrible, honey. Have you seen the doctor?" or "He shouldn't talk to you like that! He has no idea how hard you work!" et cetera.

Unfortunately, the old lady on duty tonight phoned in sick, so my father's taking the calls. He asked my mother to do it but she refused. "I love you, Bill," she said, "but there's a limit."

She said it was my turn to do the dishes, but I explained that I had *way* too much homework, not to mention all those college applications. But it was hard to concentrate. People kept videophoning me to talk about the FBI raid.

Wally looked really worried.

"You love me, don't you, Tiff?" he inquired.

"Of course I do," I answered.

"And you'll always love me? No matter what?"

"Of course I—Wally, can you hold for a second?"

The Call Waiting was buzzing, and I thought it might be Campbell, who'd probably heard that I was in the raided classroom and wanted to be sure I was okay. But it was Barbie and Kendall, so I said I'd call them back.

"Some pretty weird stuff's coming down," Wally said gloomily. "My father's probably going to kill me."

"Maybe he'll just take your car away," I suggested.

Then he started moping and muttering and I had a *heck* of a time figuring out what he was saying—but it turns out that *Wally's* the one who hacked into the Defense Department!

He's scared to *death* that the FBI will find out and send him to juvie or jail, and that his dad will have to pay for all the damages: the FBI's salaries, Mr. Brewer's broken glasses, new bombs, et cetera, et cetera.

I reminded Wally that his father has *tons* of money and besides, it might be covered by his homeowner's insurance. "He really should check that out," I urged. But nothing I said seemed to comfort him.

"I didn't mean to screw things up!" he insisted. "I just wanted to see if I could get inside the system! I was just having fun!"

I'd never seen him so hysterical. This was worse than the time his new Game Boy was stolen.

"Please don't tell anyone it was me!" he begged.

I would never betray Wally. I mean, we've gone together for ten months. But I cannot—*will* not—tell a lie. Too bad he left all those "Dolfins Rule!" messages. And he made so many spelling mistakes! Which, of course, got pointed out on the national news, making Hiram Johnson High and our educational system—not to mention Wally—look pretty silly.

I guess boys just mature more slowly than girls.

He said, "Promise you'll still love me if anything happens!"

"Nothing's going to happen," I said. But I can't help thinking: If poor Wally goes to prison, who will escort me to the Homecoming Dance?

I assured him that everything was going to be fine; then he had to hang up because the FBI was there.

I called Barbie and Kendall and they got all freaked out, afraid I might be charged as an *accessory*. Which reminds me to wear my black dress to school tomorrow, with the little silver heart necklace Wally gave me.

I explained to The Girls that I had *no idea* what

Wally had been doing. Yes, he had mentioned the Defense Department, but I thought he was talking about a video game. That's all he ever talks about lately!

"Maybe you should tell your parents what's happening," Barbie suggested.

"No," I said firmly. "Everybody's overreacting. It's time for cooler heads to prevail."

But it might not be such a bad idea to call Marcy Richmond at Channel 7 and give her an exclusive interview, or maybe hold a press conference. Just to clear things up and set the record straight.

In fact, I'll give her a buzz right now. It's the least I can do for poor Wally.

Chapter Three

I miss Wally. It's like they say: You don't know what you've got until it's gone.

The FBI didn't press charges, but Wally's dad decided to send him to a special school for criminally gifted teens, in Jamaica or New Guinea, I can never remember where. We thought it was going to be like Club Med—Wally used a tanning booth before he left—but it turns out this place is like a cross between the Boy Scouts and San Quentin! They won't even let him wear his earring!

Needless to say, as soon as I learned the worst, I organized a lunchtime protest, rallying our classmates to his defense: "Give me a W! Give me an A! Give me an L-L-Y! What's that spell? Now bring Wally home or we'll raise H-E double L!" et cetera. But it didn't do any good. Wally's father wouldn't change his mind.

What hurt me most was that one minute Wally was tonight's top story; the next minute, nobody cared anymore. He was *yesterday's* news. It was shocking. None of the TV talk shows even returned my calls! I guess they're too busy interviewing psychotic hillbillies and kids who eat their parents. Why do the *jerks* always get the attention?

Which reminds me: I have *got* to write Wally a letter.

It's just hard to know what to say to him. I mean, here I am at home, having fun, driving my car and going to football games—we absolutely *squished* Sequoia—while poor Wally's marching all over the jungle, eating coconuts for lunch.

And how can I tell him about Campbell and me? That will break poor Wally's heart. He might even try to climb the electrified fence again. In his last letter, he said, "My dad says I might be home in six months. Wait for me, Tiffany." Then he said a bunch of stuff about the importance of ironing your own clothes and respecting authority, which didn't sound a *bit* like Wally. Maybe they were holding a machete over his head.

Will he really be back in six months? Can I wait that long? Senior year will almost be over by then.

It's not that I don't love Wally anymore. I do. I miss his crunchy smile and his crinkly red hair. He's like one of those cute little Rice Krispies elves! But I realize now that what we had was puppy love, a childish infatuation.

You should see Campbell in his track shorts! I sit in the bleachers and watch him practice, and every time he runs by, he waves at me! Shelby thinks *she's* going to get him, but she's out of her mind. For one thing, she already *has* a boyfriend—even though he's an idiot—and he's *not* in Jamaica. And for another, she's not Campbell's type. He's really smart. He's in the Chess Club. He's applied to Stanford—I might go there, too. Dean Schmitz said something about a deadline?—and he plans to be a doctor.

"That's wonderful," I said as we sat in his car today, drinking diet iced tea and discussing our futures. I told him about an article I'd read that said that in the years ahead, our country will be facing a critical shortage of qualified plastic surgeons. "You know," I said, "for people like my parents."

"I'd never be a plastic surgeon." Campbell scowled.

"Why not? They perform a valuable service," I insisted. "Some people get their faces burned off. Or get in wrecks. Or get really wrinkled."

"I'm going to be a gerontologist," Campbell explained. It turns out he really loves his grandma and grandpa, so he wants to be a doctor to help old people feel better. I reminded him that people *feel* better when they *look* better, and he laughed and said, "You are too much, T-Rex." What the heck is *that* supposed to mean?

I mentioned that I really love old people, too. After Gramma died, Grandpa lived with us for a while until he started banging on the bathroom door and shouting, "I have an urgent message for King John!" whenever we were in there, and getting lost all over town. So now he lives in the nursing home, and I visit when I can, but those people are scary.

"No, they're not," Campbell insisted gently. "They're just old."

So true. The more I see of Campbell, the more I know that he is the *one* for me. The Girls say I hardly even know him, but they don't understand that when you're soul mates with someone, words aren't necessary. You just *know* what the other person's thinking.

I've asked Campbell if he wants to go to the Homecoming Dance with me—I know we'll be elected King and Queen—and he said, "That's very flattering, Tiffany. I'll get back to you." So I bought the dress today. It's darling.

But I can't help feeling guilty about poor Wally. He's the only boy I've ever let kiss me. The first time we made out, our lips got so puffy we couldn't go home until the swelling went down. The night we decided to go steady, we exchanged class rings and gave each other matching hickies. Which I'll never do again: It looks so tacky. Wally and I have really grown together. He'll live forever in my memory.

I'd better write him right now before I forget.

Dearest Wally,

I am fine and hope you are, too. You know what I mean: Under the circumstances. I think of you in that place and can't believe it. How could your father be so _mean_?

Thanks for the picture of you with the shovel. It looks like you're getting a good tan!

Well, all's fine here. I was in the Macy's fashion show the other night: Gowns for the Holiday Season. I wish you could've seen me.

Another great thing: We beat Sequoia! I mean _creamed_ them! I came up with this great new skit; we do a bunch of cheers, then form a human pyramid, with me on top and Shelby at the bottom. After all, she's the biggest. My dad took pictures. I'll send some if they turn out good.

School's fine. Things have not been the same since you left. People talk about you a lot. Do you think you'll be back for graduation?

Well, that's about it for now. I love you, Wally. We'll always be friends. Remember, life is but a lesson to be learned, then we move on, like beautiful butterflies spreading our wings.

Please write back when you have the time.

Friends Forever,
Tiffany

Stop the presses! I just had a *brilliant* idea! Now I know how Einstein felt when he did whatever he did!

This journal isn't going to be just for Miss Jones and my future grandkids. It's going to be the *story of my life*! So that later on, when I'm a famous actress, people can see all the difficulties I went through to get successful, and become inspired.

Some people (like my mother) don't know what it's like to want to be *special*. You'd think she was never young. She's always wanting me to do ordinary stuff like pick up my clothes or rake the leaves. What's the point? They'll just fall down again! She says, "Tiff, why is it so important to be famous? Don't you have any other plans in mind?"

She doesn't understand that if you're alive but nobody knows it but your family, you might as well be invisible; it doesn't count. Let's face it, who do you see on TV, in the movies, on the covers of magazines? The *famous* people. And they're not raking leaves; they're not doing something boring. They're giving interviews;

they're getting awards. Which is not to say that all the unfamous people in the world aren't important. They are. We all have our roles to play on the great stage of life. Without the audience, there couldn't be stars.

I think this journal—*My Journal, Journey of a Journal*—I'll have to come up with a good title—will really open some eyes.

Chapter Four

"Get out of here! Will you just get out?"

"It's the Tiffany Spratt Show! Starring Tiffany Spratt!"

"Get out!"

"Featuring tonight's special guest star: Tiffany Spratt!"

"*Mommmmmmmmmmmm!*"

Sorry for the interruption. I was just sitting here, minding my own business, when my brother barged in.

Before I forget: Having reviewed last night's journal entry, I have *got* to remember to tuck in that tummy. Especially after dinner.

He is *such* an idiot.

But I think including episodes like that will give people some idea of the hardships I went through and encourage them on their own paths to success.

Besides, in all the celebrity autobiographies I've

ever read, the stars talk a lot about their families, and how much their loved ones helped and encouraged them or, in certain cases, nearly drove them crazy.

My childhood falls somewhere in between. My parents love me a lot and have given me tons of stuff, like they paid for my modeling and acrobatics lessons and sent me to cheerleader camp. And in junior high, when I played softball and soccer, they were always in the stands, cheering me on to victory. Many times I saw the mascara sliding down my mother's cheeks and had to wonder, was it rain or tears of joy?

They're really good parents, and I know I shouldn't complain but lately they seem so, I don't know, out of touch. They met in the Peace Corps. What can I say. Every night when my father watches the news, he practically has a nervous breakdown. "What's the world coming to? Can you believe this?" et cetera. It hurts me to see him suffer.

No matter how successful I get, my parents will always be number one in my book. Someday I'll buy them a brand-new house or at least get the kitchen cupboards refinished. They're covered with all these gummy fingerprints.

Have I mentioned that my brother was born?

I'm kind of having trouble concentrating tonight

because, while I'm recording this, I'm watching the Home Shopping Network and they're showing this incredibly *fabulous* purse that has so many compartments, the compartments have compartments, and if I don't order now, they'll all be gone, because the little number on the screen keeps clicking off how many thousands have already been sold.

I'm back. They said to allow four weeks for delivery. The other thing that's really bugging me tonight is the nasty trick Shelby played on me today. I'm beginning to wonder about her. I think she thinks *she* should be the leader of our group, not *me*, even though *I'm* the one who got voted Head Yell Leader. And who came up with **The Cannibals** idea? Now everybody at school wants to be a **Cannibal**. And that's the other thing that's ticking me off: Some people have even made fake **Cannibals** shirts! The Girls say that just shows how popular we are, but what good is it if *everyone's* a **Cannibal**?

I went up to Lisa Keene in the hall yesterday and said, "Where did you get that sweatshirt?" She said, "At the mall." I said, "You can't just wear it around like that." "Why not?" she said. "Because you're not in our group," I told her.

Lisa, that brat, laughed right in my face and said, "I hate to tell you this, Tiffany, but you don't *own* the word."

Or did she say "world"? At any rate, it's probably too late to get it trademarked.

Like I was saying, Shelby played this really mean trick on me today and why the other Girls didn't stop her, I'll never know. They were probably scared to death she'd sit on them or something.

Anyway, being a Saturday, we decided it would be fun to dress up in our nighties and PJs and put our hair up in those old-fashioned curlers and take our teddy bears and drive by the football players' houses. So we took Shelby's car, because it's a convertible, and drove by Bobby's house, and boy, did he *blush* when he saw us!

We drove around for a while, just waving to everybody and honking the horn, then suddenly Shelby says, "I don't think the brake lights are working. Tiff, would you get out and check?I don't want to get another ticket."

So I get out of the front seat and go around to the back—and the next thing I know, Shelby *hits the gas* and disappears into the traffic.

At first, it was like one of those out-of-body experiences some people have when they almost die, and they can look down and see themselves. Only in *this* case I was downtown in my shorty pajamas—the new ones, luckily—and my bunny slippers, with my hair in all these ugly pink rollers and no way to brush it out.

I could've screamed.

People walked by, smiling, and one guy said, "Isn't it a little late for Halloween?" I stayed calm by reciting the Lord's Prayer and thinking about what I would do to Shelby's hair the next time she asked me to streak it.

Finally, after what seemed like *hours*, Shelby's car pulled up beside the curb. I got in laughing, like I'd really been having fun.

"We didn't know she was going to do that!" Ashley sobbed, and the other Girls agreed, and I believe them.

"Sorry," Shelby said. "I was just kidding."

"Oh, it was too funny!" I said. "You should've seen the looks on people's faces!"

"You should've seen yours." Shelby smirked.

So we all laughed some more, after Ashley stopped crying, then we drove to the mall, and Shelby treated me to an ice cream cone, orange sherbet and chocolate chiffon. But she's *nuts* if she thinks that settles it. Tiffany Spratt does not forget. Tiffany Spratt bides her time.

♥ ♥ ♥

Have I said enough stuff about my family? I guess I can always add more later, about how they've supported and encouraged me, et cetera. I just wish my mother would try to see things from *my* point of view. She was in here a while ago, complaining about the way I'd done the dishes.

"You didn't even scrape off the food!" she said. "We could serve the plates as leftovers!" et cetera.

She keeps bugging me about doing my homework. Haven't my grades always been fine? She looks me over so coolly sometimes, as if she's wondering what I'd sell for by the pound.

Hey, that's a pretty good line! Miss Jones always says I'm a lazy writer. She's really being tight about my famous women essay. She won't let me write about Little Tina. She'd never even *heard* of Little Tina!

I explained that Little Tina has a TV talk show, a gold record, a best-selling book—*SHORT BUT SWEET: The Little Tina Story*—her own line of active sports and underwear, et cetera. But Miss Jones said no; she meant someone like Margaret Walker, our first woman president, or that lady who went to Mars, people like that. I know they were important, but for heaven's sake, they're dead! Miss Jones just doesn't get it.

She reminds me of my mother, going on and on about my potential. Don't they realize I realize how intelligent I am? I could've graduated early and got going on my career, but then I wouldn't have gotten to be Head Yell Leader or graduate with all of my friends.

Sometimes when I think about graduation night, my eyes begin to prickle with tears. Like right now, as I picture leaving my classmates and teachers behind, and we go our separate ways into the future.

First, of course, there'll be a beautiful ceremony. The Girls and I will lead the official school cheer. A bunch of people will give inspiring speeches. Then the choir will sing a beautiful song, maybe that new one of Little Tina's, as our hearts swell with Dolphin pride and memories.

And then it will be time to say good-bye.

Good-bye, hallowed halls of Hiram Johnson High! Good-bye, dear friends and Senior Quad and Snak Shak! Good-bye to all those happy times!

I just wish school wasn't so boring.

Chapter Five

I should hold a daily news conference or hand out press releases or something, so people will know what's going on in my life. I have to keep *explaining* everything!

No, Wally and I have *not* broken up. It's just that we've agreed that we should see other people while he's gone. Which I'm sure he *would* agree with if he could write or call me. He's on restriction. All because he got on the phone one night and tried to hire a lawyer.

But, like I told him the last time I wrote, "We'll always be together in our hearts." Too bad Shelby sent him that picture of me and Cannibal, I mean Campbell, being crowned King and Queen of the Homecoming Dance.

It was such a *glorious* night! The Girls and I rented a white limousine, and we felt like movie stars or something! Then we picked up the boys and they kind of wrecked everything by arguing about how much the limo cost and saying why should *they* have to pay; *we* were the ones who rented it, et cetera.

Then Campbell said—and I could've kissed him on the spot—"Come on, guys. Let's not spoil the evening."

So the boys agreed to pay for it. But I'll never understand why Shelby goes with that cheapskate Bryan. He wanted to take us to Smorgas Bob's for dinner!

I explained to him that Smorgas Bob's was out of the question; that we already had reservations at Les Chattes, in his name, and if we didn't show up, they'd charge him anyway. So we went to Les Chattes, but he was a bad sport about it, pretended to burp all through dinner, et cetera.

That's another thing I admire about Campbell. He never thinks burps are funny. I thought I was going to lose my *mind* when Ronnie kept talking about his socks! I'm sorry, but I don't want to hear about anyone's stinky feet, *especially* while I'm eating dinner.

Anyway, the evening could not have been more perfect! The deejay played all of my favorite songs, and Campbell is a fabulous dancer. Which is not to say anything against poor Wally, who just pushes you around like a shopping cart. When I complimented Campbell on his dancing, he laughed and said his mom made him take lessons in junior high. Talk about an all-around athlete! Track, basketball, swim team. He even knows how to do karate! I asked him if he'd show me some moves sometime, and he smiled and said, "We'll see."

But the thing I love most about Campbell is his modesty. When we got elected King and Queen, he actually looked surprised! Like he doesn't even know how gorgeous he is! I mean, not just his looks, but inside, where it counts.

Everyone clapped and threw confetti, and Mr. Brewer took our pictures for the yearbook. The night was like some wonderful dream come true, so perfect that it made me feel humble, like, too bad more people can't have my life. But then I guess it wouldn't be so special.

After the dance I drove Campbell home, but first we stopped here for some hot chocolate. My brother was watching TV but I told him to get lost, and my folks were already in bed, thank heaven. I made hot chocolate, then we went into the TV room and talked. One thing I don't get: When I'm trying to be funny, he just *looks* at me; and when I'm being real serious about stuff, he laughs.

We were sitting close together on the sofa, and I was thinking he'd put his arm around me, but he just kept watching this dumb old war movie.

I guess I must've sighed.

Campbell looked at me. "You must really miss Wally," he said gently.

"Yes," I answered. Which in a way is true, but not what I wanted to discuss at that time.

"Have you heard from him lately?"

"No," I said. "He's on restriction."

I explained that Wally can't write letters or use the phone for a whole month, and that they're making him do a bunch of extra chores, like go out into the exercise yard and clean up after all the monkeys.

"That sounds pretty rough," Campbell said.

My eyes filled with tears. But I have to be honest: Was I crying for poor Wally or for myself?

"I'm glad I could be there for you tonight, Tiff," Campbell said. "You've really been there for me, too. It's not easy being the new kid at school."

I thought for sure he'd take my hand then, but he didn't. Then suddenly I realized: Campbell's like the guy in this stupid movie who threw himself on the bomb to save his friends! Campbell would *never* steal another guy's girlfriend! He's too true-blue and loyal— and he doesn't even *know* Wally!

I *really* started crying then. Good thing my mascara was waterproof. Campbell took me in his arms and tenderly held me.

He said, "I'm sorry you're so sad, Tiff. I know this is hard on you."

"Sort of," I admitted.

"Don't worry," he said. "Wally will be back soon."

How could I explain that, although in a way I still love Wally, I really love *him*, too?

"You're so nice, Campbell," I said.

"So are you, T-Rex," he answered.

What *is* it with this T-Rex business? "Campbell, there's something I have to tell you," I began. "Wally and I—"

"Oh, hi, Mrs. Spratt."

I couldn't believe it! My *mother* was standing in the doorway. In her nightgown! The yucky one the cat likes to suck on. Talk about bad timing!

"Hi, kids," she said. "Did you have fun tonight?"

"Yes, it was great," Campbell said. "You're looking at the King and Queen of the Homecoming Dance."

"Really!" she said. "That must've been exciting. Tiffany, are you all right?"

"She's sad about Wally," Campbell explained gently. "She wished he could've been there tonight."

"Hmmm," my mother said.

I said, "I guess I'm just tired."

"Yes, it's getting late." Campbell stood and pulled me to my feet. "Tiff, would you see me to the door?"

I wanted to see my *mother* to the door. Campbell's hand was strong and warm. I followed him meekly.

"I can give you a ride home," I offered.

"No, thanks," he said. "I'll walk. It's a beautiful night."

"The most beautiful night of my life," I said meaningfully.

Campbell leaned down, and I thought: *This is it!* But instead, he just kissed me on the forehead.

"Good night, Queenie. I'll see you on Monday."

And before I could speak, he was gone, fading into the darkness like a falling star, like a beautiful dream at dawn.

Chapter Six

It's over. Cannibal and I have broken up.

I can't believe it, but it's true.

I've been crying so much my eyes are all puckered up.

Behold: the face of tragedy.

Maybe I should—no, I was just thinking maybe I should fix myself up a little before I record my journal entry tonight. But why hide the truth? Why pretend? Just let me get rid of these raccoon eyes. . . .

That's better. All of The Girls have been calling. I've got such great friends! The best friends in the whole wide world! Ashley and Kendall said not to worry; they think everything will turn out fine. Barbie says I'm too good for Campbell. She's going to call him up and bawl him out. And Shelby said my face looked puffy, and that if I dab a little Preparation H around my eyes, it will really bring the swelling down.

I found some in my dad's medicine chest, but then I started wondering, is it *true* or just another weird joke that Shelby's playing and I'll end up with a permanent *squint*?

I can't go to school tomorrow looking like this. I've never been so sad in my whole *life*! I keep picturing Campbell's angry face. No one's *ever* looked at me like that before. Besides my mother, of course.

It all started when we were having lunch today. We were sitting in my favorite booth at the Hot Spot, and I'd ordered the cheeseburger with fries and a chocolate milk. Then the girl asked Cannibal, I mean Campbell— I am so *upset*!—for his order, and he said a Gardenburger.

I said, "What the heck's that? Made out of worms and dirt?" And Campbell smiled and said, "No, it's made out of cereal and vegetables."

So that was fine, and we were joking and laughing and I was sitting there thinking how handsome he is, but not *too* handsome, so rugged and strong, when I suddenly realized he'd stopped talking.

"I'm sorry," I apologized. "What were you saying?"

"I said sometimes I get the feeling you're not listening to me, Tiff."

"That's not true," I insisted. I practically hang on his every word! "I was just looking at you."

"Well, do you think you could listen at the same time?" he asked.

"Sure."

We laughed and it seemed like everything was fine; then the waitress brought our orders. And that's when things went to heck in a bucket of chicken.

Looking back, I think maybe Campbell's right. Maybe I *am* blind and living in a world of my own, because the signs had been there all along, but I wouldn't let myself see them. Because it seemed like we were made for each other, and things had been going so perfect.

I asked if he wanted a bite of my burger and he said, "No, thanks," and I said, "Are you sure?" because his burger was flat and kind of gray and mine was so nice and red and juicy.

That's when he told me, and I was so *shocked*, I thought I must've misunderstood him.

"You can't be a vet." I smiled. "You're still in high school."

As usual, he thought I was trying to be funny! Then he said, "No, Tiff. Not a veterinarian. A *vegetarian*. I don't eat meat."

I realize now that I should've kept my mouth shut, but I laughed and said, "You're kidding! I've never even *met* a vegetarian before! You mean like, what, for health reasons?"

"Not really," he said, calmly chomping. "I don't eat anything that has a face."

"My burger doesn't have a face, you silly!"

"No," Campbell said, "but the cow did."

I thought I was going to vomit through my *nose*. I'd never heard anything so *disgusting*! It was like he was calling me a *murderer* or something!

"What about fish?"

"Fish have faces," he said.

"Yes," I said, "but they look like—fish!"

"Tiffany, why are you getting so upset?"

"I'm not upset!" I said. I'd torn my napkin into shreds. Shelby and Bryan came in just then, so I tossed the shreds into the air like confetti and laughed, but my heart was breaking. Why did Campbell have to turn out to be a *nut*? Why hadn't I seen this coming? I should've guessed the other night, when we went out after the show, and he wouldn't even *try* the chicken fingers— even after I'd explained that they weren't really fingers!

"You can eat whatever you want," he said. "But look at it from an environmental standpoint, too. It took tons of grain to grow that burger, and cow poop is a major pollutant."

"That's hardly the point!" I whispered furiously. Shelby and Bryan were sitting nearby. "I just don't want you to be one of those people!"

"What people?" he said.

"The kind that thinks animals have rights!"

"They do," he said.

"I can't *believe* this! Why didn't you tell me sooner!"

"Tell you what?" Campbell's face was getting red. "I've mentioned it before, but you probably weren't listening. It's like you're living in your own little world."

"That's not true!" I denied.

"And another thing," he said, "why do you keep calling me Cannibal? You can't even remember my name."

"If you're going to pick on every little thing I do—"

"I'm trying to be honest with you, Tiff," he said. "Don't you want to be real friends?"

"Of *course* I do," I said. "But why can't you be like everybody else?"

"Millions of people all over the world are vegetarians!"

"Yes, but they're not Americans!" I pointed out.

"Tiffany, you're not making any sense," he said.

"Neither are you!" I said. "What about Noah's Ark? If God didn't want us to eat meat, He wouldn't have given us all those animals!"

"It was called Noah's Ark, not Noah's Diner," Campbell said.

My mind reeled with shock as Campbell kept talking. He said I shouldn't buy any products from companies that do animal testing—products I have to use every day, like deodorant and mascara and shampoo!

"Are you saying that animals are more important than *us*?"

"I've got news for you, Tiff. We *are* animals," he said.

How could Campbell be so *irrational*?

I said, "The next thing you know, you'll be having protests, or freeing all the cats in Biology Lab!"

"It's a little late for that; they're dead," Campbell snapped. "But I wouldn't dissect one. Mimi Durning and I went to the library instead."

"You went to the library with *Mimi Durning*?" I gasped. "Now everyone will think you're a weirdo, too!"

"Why, because I don't want to play with dead cats? What's the matter with you, Tiff? You're too smart to act dumb. Do you always have to be so superficial?"

I almost slugged him. But I could feel Shelby watching us with her greedy little eyes. The *last* thing I wanted to do was argue with my boyfriend in public!

"You see?" Campbell said. "You're doing it right now."

"Doing what?" I demanded.

"You care more about what Shelby thinks than what I'm saying."

"That's not true!" I said.

"Then why are you smiling?"

"I'm not smiling!" I insisted.

"Yes, you are."

I felt my lips. The corners were turned up! I thought I was going to freak out!

"Campbell, you don't understand," I stammered. "I'm too upset to talk to you right now. Maybe I'll phone you later."

"Whatever." He threw down his napkin and stalked out. He didn't even recycle his soda can! He just left it right there on the table!

I couldn't go back to class. I drove home and collapsed on my bed, crying. My father heard me and knocked on my door.

"Honey," he said, looking worried, "what's wrong?"

"Nothing, Daddy," I told him. "It's just cramps."

He must've called my mother because she came home early. She sat beside me on the bed and said, "Tiffany, what's the matter?"

"Oh, nothing!" I sobbed. "My whole life is ruined, that's all."

She stroked my back. "Is it really that bad?"

I was crying so hard I could barely talk. "Campbell and I—" Then the tears overwhelmed me.

"Did you and Campbell have a fight?" she asked.

"Yes," I managed. "We broke up! It's over!"

She said, "I didn't know you two were going steady."

How can my mother be so *blind*? "He's the only person I've ever really loved," I moaned.

"Honey, you two hardly know each other," she said. "Don't you think you might be overreacting?"

"Mom, you don't understand!" I wept. "Today I found out that Campbell . . . that Campbell . . ." I could hardly bear to say the words, "that Campbell is a vegetarian!"

"So?"

"So why does he have to be one of those people? Everybody I know eats meat!"

"I don't," she said.

"Since when?" I asked.

"Two years ago."

I guess I hadn't noticed. The important thing was that Campbell and I were through. My beautiful dream of our future was shattered. How could we get married and go out to dinner with our friends if Campbell was going to ask the waitress if there was anything without a *face* on the menu? How can someone who looks so *normal* be such a *radical*?

My mother said, "Maybe you'll feel better after you eat something."

"What's for dinner?" I asked.

"Tuna fish casserole."

I tried to eat, but it was like everything on the plate was staring *back* at me. So I came upstairs and lay down on my bed. The horrible scene at the Hot Spot kept replaying in my head. Perhaps my mother was right and I'd overreacted. After all, it's a free country. Campbell's entitled to his opinion, no matter how stupid it is.

But it's too late now, too late for apologies. Campbell will probably never speak to me again.

A miracle just happened! My brother came to the door and said I had a phone call.

It was Campbell! He said, "I tried to call you, but your line was busy, so I called your folks' number."

I admitted I'd left my phone off the hook.

"If you'd rather not talk—" he began.

"That's okay," I said. For once, I was glad he doesn't have a videophone and couldn't see how bad I looked. "We're going to have to face it sometime."

"I'm sorry about what happened today, Tiff. I really am," he said. "I shouldn't have called you superficial."

"That's okay," I said, happy tears welling in my eyes. "I shouldn't have called you a weirdo."

"I don't want to fight with you, Tiff," he said. "It makes me feel so bad. But sometimes it seems like you're putting on an act, when all you have to do is be yourself."

"I know. I want you to be yourself, too," I said.

"Real friends don't have to agree about everything," he pointed out. "Real friends can accept each other's differences."

"That's true," I agreed. I want Campbell and me to be *more* than friends, but it wasn't the time to go into all that. "It's just that you're so important to me, Campbell," I added.

"Well, at least you got my name right," he said.

We laughed. It felt so *good* to be together again!

Then Campbell started talking about the importance of accepting people for who they really are, with all their uniqueness and warts, et cetera, and how, if we all lived by the Golden Rule, this world would be heaven on Earth and so on; then the Call Waiting buzzed, so I put him on hold.

It was Shelby. She said, "Did you hear the news?"

"What news?" I said.

"They're going to make a movie at our school!" she said.

"You're *kidding*!"

"No!"

"Are you *sure*?" I demanded.

"Absolutely," she said. "Amber Johnson was working in the attendance office and she heard Principal Brown talking to the movie people."

"I can't *believe* it!" I said. "This is so fantastic!"

I told Campbell I'd have to call him back.

Chapter Seven

Rumors about the movie were flying all over school this morning, and I thought for sure the principal would announce it over the PA. But it was just the usual boring news: Don't forget the freshman car wash, bring in canned goods for the homeless, et cetera.

I was *dying* of suspense, so I tried to sneak out, but Mr. Brewer's sub was being really tight; she wouldn't even let me go to the bathroom! What if I'd really had to go? And who knows when Mr. Brewer will be back. The other day while he was instructing Becki Jordan in the Drivers' Ed car, somebody cut in front of them and Mr. Brewer *snapped*. He made Becki *chase* the guy, and when he stopped for a light, Mr. Brewer jumped out and *attacked* him!

Anyway, while I was sitting there wondering how I could find out what was happening, Amber Johnson came in with a message from Dean Schmitz: He wanted to see me right away! Talk about perfect timing! Thank you, God!

In the hall I asked Amber if the rumors were true, and she said the movie people were in Principal Brown's office right then!

I made a quick stop in the bathroom to check my hair. It looked great. Then I walked past the secretary—she said, "You can't go in there, Tiffany"—and into Principal Brown's office.

"I'm sorry," I apologized, when everybody stared at me. "I'm looking for Dean Schmitz."

"Have you tried his office, Tiffany?" the principal asked.

You could tell the people were from Hollywood. The man was wearing sunglasses—in the office!—and the woman was thin and dressed in black. I shook their hands and introduced myself.

"Hello," I said. "I'm Tiffany Spratt." That *Spratt* has *got* to go. "Head Yell Leader at Hiram Johnson High School. Welcome to our campus."

"Thank you, Tiffany. That will be all," the principal said.

"I understand you're making a movie at our school," I continued. "That's *so* exciting! Are you working from a screenplay or a treatment?" Thank *God* for my subscription to *People* magazine!

54

"A treatment," the man answered, impressed. "Have you had much film experience?"

"Not really," I admitted, "but I'm a professional model, and my goal is to be a TV and movie actress."

"Thank you, Tiffany," the principal said. "You can go back to class now."

"What kind of modeling have you done?" the woman asked me.

"Runway and print," I said. "I can show you my portfolio."

"Bring it to the auditions," she suggested.

"I will," I promised. "What's the movie called?"

"*Scream Bloody Murder.* It's a comedy."

"I can really scream," I said.

"That won't be necessary, Tiffany." Principal Brown butted in again. "As I've explained to Ms. Stuart and Mr. Goldman, we're running a school here, not a movie set."

"But just think what an educational experience it would be for our students," I pointed out. "And it would really put Hiram Johnson on the map!"

"I fail to see how a murder movie is educational," grumped Principal Brown. What an old sourpuss he was being! Doesn't he realize that when opportunity knocks, you at *least* have to open the door?

"As I've explained, Mr. Brown," said Mr. Goldman,

"nothing's written in stone. We're willing to work with your people on the script. And remember, none of the murders actually take place on campus."

"Except for the one in the cafeteria," Ms. Stuart noted. "When the cook gets possessed and serves the poisoned tapioca."

"True," said Mr. Goldman, "but only the fat kid dies."

"And the scene where the maintenance man goes berserk," Ms. Stuart added, "and mows down all those kids."

"Sure," said Mr. Goldman, "but with a lawn mower, not a gun."

"No, no, no." Principal Brown shook his head. "The custodians won't go for that. And the school board would never approve it."

"Have the board members seen the treatment?" I asked.

"No they haven't, Tiffany, but—is there some reason why you're still here?"

"Well, shouldn't they be allowed to make up their own minds?" I asked. "After all, *they're* the ones running the school district. Maybe they could play themselves in the movie!"

"That's a possibility," Mr. Goldman said.

Principal Brown was making an *awful* face, so I addressed Ms. Stuart and Mr. Goldman. "Why don't you make a presentation at the next school board meeting?" I suggested. "I'll rally all the kids to show support! We'll work together as a team to achieve our goal and score another victory for Hiram Johnson! Oh, please don't turn us down, Mr. Brown! This is the chance of a lifetime!"

There were tears in my eyes. Even *I* was surprised. Everybody was staring at me, frozen.

"Thank you, Tiffany," the principal said. "Go back to class now. Or wherever you were going."

I gave Ms. Stuart and Mr. Goldman my phone number and told them I'd be glad to help in any way I could.

Ms. Stuart asked about my **Cannibals** sweatshirt. I explained that The Girls and I were in a gang. Not a gang, per se, more like a club. Mr. Goldman seemed really interested.

"Maybe we could work that into the script," he said. "I mean, what could be worse than cannibal vampires?"

Ms. Stuart looked doubtful. "I don't know, Alex," she said. "If the vampires eat their victims, there won't be any new vampires. That's the problem."

"I see what you mean," he said. "We can work that out later. Tiffany, it's been a pleasure."

I shook hands with them again—but not with Principal Brown; he looked like he wanted to bite off my fingers—and floated out of the office on a golden cloud.

Me! In a real Hollywood movie! Maybe even helping to write the script!

Unfortunately, Dean Schmitz ran out of his office and grabbed my arm.

"I sent for you a half hour ago!" he said. "Where have you been?"

"I'm sorry, Dean Schmitz, but I can't talk now," I said. "When is the next school board meeting?"

"Right after the holidays," he answered. "Tiffany, do you intend to graduate with your class or are you planning to stay on as a janitor?"

"I'm sorry, Dean Schmitz, but I have to go home."

"Oh, please don't tell me it's cramps again!" he blared. "You have more cramps than the entire NFL."

I couldn't believe it! Why not blab it all over the whole school so *everyone* can hear?

I leaned close to his hairy ear and whispered, "Clots."

He reared back as if I'd spit at him.

I ran into Campbell in the Senior Quad. "Did you hear the news?" I asked.

"What news?" he said.

"About the movie they're filming on campus!" I said. "Isn't it great?"

"I guess."

Sometimes I have to wonder about Campbell. I mean, I know he lived in LA and everything, but you'd think he'd be happy that I'm finally getting my big break.

"I'll probably get a part, being a model and all," I said. "They'll need people with experience and talent."

"Modeling's not exactly a talent," Campbell said. Then he started—it was *horrible*—going through all these poses.

"Look, I'm running in place," he said. "Now I'm laughing." He threw back his head and grinned. "Now I'm thinking: Hmmmm." He frowned and cupped his chin. "Now I'm waving to someone. Now I'm throwing a football—"

In the two months we've been going together, I have *never* been so angry at him.

I said, "I'm sorry you think my whole life is such a joke."

"I don't. It's just that I've done that number."

"You never told me you modeled."

"Yes, I did," he said. "It just got too absurd."

"What do you mean?" I asked him.

"I like to smile when I feel like smiling. Not when somebody tells me to," he said.

Sometimes I think Campbell tries to get too deep. Why can't he just relax and *enjoy* life?

He offered to walk me to math, but I explained that I had to get home right away; I had *tons* of work to do before the next school board meeting.

"What kind of work?" he asked.

I promised to tell him later. And even though he'd ticked me off with all those silly poses, I kissed his cheek to show there were no hard feelings.

My dad was using the computer when I got home, but I explained that I had an urgent school project. I just can't say enough about the Internet. It is truly the gateway to the future. I know it got poor Wally into trouble—I wonder how he's doing—but it puts the whole world at your fingertips. It's like going inside God's brain.

Plus, computers make writing so fast and easy! In the old days, people had to use typewriters or even pencils, and that could take forever.

So here is something very important I want to say

to all of my future readers: These days, you have *got* to be computer literate. The computer is a *very* important tool. Stay in school, study hard, and go to college. And whatever you do, learn *marketable* job skills. Like Miss Jones says, "He (or she) who fails to prepare prepares to fail."

Even if you're planning on a career in show business like I am, let's face it: Dreams don't always come true. So if you want to act or model, ask yourself, and be honest: How beautiful or handsome *am* I, really? Lots of people apply to model at Macy's who, truthfully, don't stand a chance. You want to just go up to them and say, "Don't take this wrong. I don't mean to hurt your feelings, but this is *never* going to happen."

It's sad.

In no time at all surfing the Net, I'd collected a wealth of information—Remember: She who fails to prepare prepares to fail!—showing how much money a movie company typically pumps into the local economy when it chooses that town for a location: how many residents are employed as carpenters, caterers, extras, et cetera; the number of hotel and motel rooms the movie people rent, not to mention all the meals they eat in restaurants; *plus* the money from all the tourists who later flock to the famous town to see where the movie got made. Sometimes the movie company even makes *permanent improvements* that the people in the town get to keep!

The track regraded? The cafeteria repainted? A new school board meeting room?

Barbie and Kendall called, but I couldn't talk; I was on the phone with the chamber of commerce.

Chapter Eight

It's funny how, when things are really boring, you've got all the time in the world for your journal, but nothing to talk about; and when things are going really *good* you're too busy to get it all down.

Oh, well, that's life!

We had a very Merry Christmas, in *spite* of the fact that my brother left the front door unlocked and Grandpa took off and we couldn't find him. The police brought him back in time for Christmas dinner, but he was having trouble eating and it turned out he was wearing somebody else's teeth! Daddy got mad and called the home, and they got mad at *him* and said that Grandpa's been stealing *everybody's* teeth; they found a whole *pile* of them under his pillow. So now they have to figure out whose teeth are whose, which apparently is a big honking mess.

Luckily, Grandpa didn't seem too upset; he kept

gnawing on a turkey leg until my mother couldn't stand it anymore and brought him a bowl of ice cream.

It being the holiday season, 1-800-YOR-MAMA was extra busy, so my father asked my mother to take some calls. Which she wouldn't, of course, even though it was Christmas. So he changed his voice to an old lady's again, which works out amazingly well since the callers do most of the talking.

I got some really nice gifts: clothes, music, books, a new TV, et cetera, even though my mother had *insisted* that we were cutting back this year because the holiday has become a *spending orgy.* She says that people have way more stuff than they need, and we should give everything to the poor. Like a homeless person needs a TV set. I know my mother means well, but sometimes she doesn't think things through.

I gave Campbell a bottle of this fabulous new, very expensive aftershave called Urge. So he wouldn't think I was being cheap, I "forgot" to remove the price tag. Fifty dollars. He gave me a piece of paper that showed he'd donated ten dollars in my name to an organization that rescues abandoned pet ferrets. Later, when The Girls asked what he'd given me, I smiled and said, "I'd rather not say." Which was true.

I did not forget my poor darling Wally. Apparently

he's developed some kind of allergy to manioc, or manatee root, or whatever it is he's been eating, so I sent him some Tums in Christmas colors, insect repellent, an honorary **Cannibals** sweatshirt, and the fashion layout from the *San Francisco Chronicle*, starring yours truly in the Macy's Holiday Magic Show.

If only he could've been there! That would've really cheered him up! The Girls and I have never looked more elegant, more "swannay," as Mr. Margo, who's in charge of the fashion shows, said. Even Shelby looked stunning, in spite of the fact that she's been hitting the pork rinds pretty hard lately. Also, her legs looked like she'd given them a *mohawk*! I realize that we were wearing long gowns, but you'd think she'd have enough *pride* in herself to do a thorough job of shaving! I mean, nobody sees your underwear, either, but don't you feel better when it's clean?

But the holiday season wasn't just an endless round of parties, fashion, and fun. There were school papers to write—I have *got* to get mine done!—Christmas shopping; organizing support for *Scream Bloody Murder*; and last but not least, singing Christmas carols at a local nursing home. Definitely *not* my grandpa's; he always says the darnedest things to me. Like, "Midge, tell Fred to get the lead out!" I love him and all, but that's really unnerving.

Our Christmas caroling visit was a trying, but extremely worthwhile, experience for me and The Girls, even though Ashley completely freaked out when an old lady in a wheelchair grabbed her and wouldn't let go.

"Omigod," she sobbed when she finally stopped screaming. "They should film the movie here! This place is creepy!"

I explained to Ashley that there is nothing "creepy" about getting old; that's simply what happens when people let themselves go. She said, "Well, couldn't they just wear Face-Its or something?" Face-Its are these little adhesive strips that pull up your skin like a mini-face-lift. Most people wear the invisible flesh-tone kind, but others prefer the "bold mode" that sparkle with color and glitter.

I explained to Ashley that it was a little late for Face-Its at the nursing home. For one thing, they'd have to be industrial strength. And for another, wouldn't it look a little weird if everybody there was *smiling*? I mean, what have they got to smile about? They're practically dying! I wish my mother would use Face-Its, but she won't, even though they'd make her look ten years younger, especially if she'd wear more scarfs. Her neck looks like Toby the Turtle's.

So The Girls and I really got into the spirit of giving, which is why it bugs me that some people think teenagers care only about themselves. Which isn't true. And even though I've got so much on my mind: modeling, the movie, Campbell, Wally, school, et cetera, I can never let it show on my face. My job as a model is to radiate poise and beauty—and, of course, make the clothes look great.

Something I'd like to say right now to all those people like Campbell who think that modeling is a joke: Try running up a fake staircase in an evening gown, then holding up your skirt so your designer shoes will show. Or posing for photographs for hours while you're facing a fan so it looks like the breeze is blowing your hair. The fan completely dries out your nasal passages. You have to go home and soak your nose.

So don't tell *me* that being a model doesn't take talent! It takes much more than beauty and talent—it takes the will to survive.

I'm back. This phone never stops ringing! Everybody's so excited about the school board meeting tonight. Campbell called to see how I was feeling, then got in a big tizzy when I told him I'd put him on speakerphone so I could videotape us talking. He said I should've asked his permission, that I'd violated his privacy and his constitutional rights. You'd think I was working for the CIA! You can't even see him, only me, so what's the problem? He made me promise to edit him out, but my fingers were crossed and I know he'll thank me later.

Maybe I was being a bit crabby myself. The truth is, I'm a little nervous about the school board meeting. I'll have to get up and make a presentation in front of all those people—including the movie people, kind of like an audition—but also because—and this is the part that kills me—my *mother*, the president of the Teachers' Association, is leading the protest *against* the movie! Talk about when worlds collide.

When it became clear that we were on different sides, I was afraid she'd take it out on me at home and maybe ground me for a year or act real stinky. But after several bitter arguments at the dinner table, we agreed to not discuss the matter anymore. I just hope she's not a bad sport when my side wins. Which I know we will. I've done my homework, I've made the phone calls. All the numbers are on my side. She just keeps talking about the "commercialization of education"— as if it was a real bad thing! Like when she tried to stop the Pepsi company from donating shirts to our football players. So *what* if the shirts say "Drink Pepsi"? It's not like the players have it tattooed on their heads!

My mother is so naive sometimes. I just hope that what happens at the meeting tonight doesn't crush her.

Scream Bloody Murder! Our team wins! I hate to say it, but we *smushed* her!

Usually the board members refer to my mother as "Beth," and it's all very friendly and informal. But tonight, things were different, maybe because the place was *packed*, with kids and parents spilling into the hallway, and the TV and newspaper reporters I'd called.

The Girls and I wore our **Cannibal** sweatshirts, and a bunch of kids were wearing the fake ones. It took all my self-control not to rip them off.

The board members were acting stiff and self-conscious, and they called my mother Ms. Bennett-Spratt. And for reasons I will *never* understand, my mother hadn't even fixed her hair; just piled it on her head like a bad hat. She was even wearing the same dress she wore to school today! I mean, I wasn't expecting an evening gown, but didn't she realize what was at stake?

When it was her turn to speak, she talked about the prevalence of drugs, violence, and sex in our culture, and how the teachers don't feel we should sell out our campus just so somebody can make a fast buck. She went on and on and *on* about the importance of education.

"Some things are more important than money," she said.

"Name one!" somebody shouted. People laughed.

It was pitiful.

Campbell wasn't there. I'd asked him to come and give me support, but he said he'd volunteered at the Boys & Girls Club and wasn't about to flake out. "Couldn't you go some other time?" I begged, but he refused. Which was very disappointing, although I admire his commitment very much.

Anyway, to make a long story short, the movie people, who looked *incredibly* cool, got up and made a speech about what a wonderful opportunity this was for Hiram Johnson, and how our school and town would really benefit. Mrs. Thornton raised a question about filming "objectionable" scenes on campus. "You must understand," she told the movie people, "that as a board trustee, I have a grave responsibility, et cetera, et cetera."

Ms. Stuart and Mr. Goldman assured her that the board's concerns would be taken into consideration and that nothing was written in stone. They asked if she'd be interested in playing herself in the movie. Mrs. Thornton blushed and said she might, and everybody clapped except the teachers.

Then some parents got up and complained about glorifying sex and drugs, but Mr. Goldman explained that any teens in the movie who had fun would be killed. Then other parents said, "Come on, people! Where's your sense of humor? We're talking about a movie, not real life!" et cetera.

Finally, it was my turn to speak. And when those hundreds of eyes were fastened on me, and I laid out my facts and graphs and figures, I could *feel*, like warm waves bathing my body, the tide of public opinion turning in my favor. It reminded me of that old show my dad likes, *Perry Mason*. And I was Perry Mason and my mother was poor old Hamilton Burger, losing yet another case she thought she could win; arguing with the movie people and yes-butting the school board, while the other teachers chimed in.

It made me feel sad and a little uncomfortable, and I wanted to put my arms around her and tell her better luck next time, but the timing wasn't right.

Then the school board voted four to one to allow *Scream Bloody Murder* to be filmed on campus!

♥ ♥ ♥

I'd ridden with The Girls, so Shelby drove me home. When I walked in, I was afraid my mother might jump out and stab me, or be really mad, or acting weird. But she wasn't—except for the fact that she was out on the patio, smoking a cigarette. She hasn't smoked in years.

"No hard feelings?" I called through the glass between us.

She looked puzzled and cupped her ear.

"No hard feelings!" I shouted. "Are you all right?"

She smiled and said something I couldn't hear, her words blocked by the invisible wall between us. It was like watching her on TV with the sound turned off.

Chapter Nine

I had a *very* unpleasant discussion with Miss Jones today. Sometimes she says the strangest things. Like today she said, "God help me, I'm very fond of you, Tiff." Was that supposed to be a compliment?

First off, she gave me detention after school, in spite of the fact that I needed to get home right away and practice my screaming for the audition tomorrow. *Plus*, that made me miss my appointment with Marge to get my hair trimmed and highlighted.

Then she made a really big deal about the fact that I'd been a tiny bit late handing in my "What Freedom Means to Me" essay.

I explained to Miss Jones that my schedule has been hectic; that I practically need a secretary to keep track of my meetings, modeling assignments, Pep Squad practices, and games, et cetera.

She said, "That's all very interesting, Tiff, but you've got to get your priorities straight."

What does she think I'm *trying* to do?

"And this essay." She picked it up as if it were written on *toilet* paper. "'What freedom means to me is my new car'? Tiffany, I was referring to the personal liberties we enjoy as Americans."

"It's an American car," I pointed out. Is it *my* fault she didn't explain the assignment clearly?

She was still looking annoyed, so I admitted that I have been experiencing some personal difficulties lately. Life on the home front has been *tense*. For one thing, Grandpa keeps escaping from the nursing home and Daddy has to drive all over town with that silly loudspeaker, trying to find him: *"Dad! Bill Spratt! Billy Boy, where are you? Front and center, soldier! Dinner's on the table!"* et cetera.

He drove by school one day when I was standing outside and somebody said, "Tiffany, isn't that your father?"

"I don't think so," I said, but he spotted me and boomed, "Hi, Tiffy! Have you seen your grandpa?"

Luckily, Grandpa can't get far in those slippers.

Also, my mother is being impossible. The other night when I came out of the bathroom, she said, "How many times do you wash your hair?"

"What do you mean?" I said.

"Each time you wash it," she said. "How many times do you shampoo?"

"Twice," I answered.

"Why?" she persisted. Her eyes were glittering.

"Because it says to on the bottle."

"Your hair's not clean after the first shampoo?"

"I don't know," I said, afraid she was having a menopausal meltdown. "It says on the bottle to shampoo twice."

"Exactly!" She clapped her hands and grinned. "So you'll use it up faster and have to buy more!"

"It's just shampoo," I said. "We can afford it."

"That's not the point! Why shampoo twice? Why not shampoo a *hundred* times?" she roared. "Don't you see what's happening, Tiff? You're being brainwashed with a creme rinse!"

I think the problem is my brother. He's driving her crazy. He and his friends have started a band called The Glands, and unfortunately, he's the drummer. He practices in his room and pounds the drums so hard you can feel them in your teeth.

I wonder if I've mentioned his name. It's Ricardo. But I couldn't pronounce that when I was little, so I still call him what I did when we were kids. Retardo.

I thought hearing about all my personal problems would make Miss Jones more understanding. She's usually so sensitive and sweet. But she told me I have to do the essay over or I'll get an Incomplete!

So now I'm supposed to make time for *that* when what I *really* should be doing is writing poor Wally a letter. He sent me a picture of him in his official **Cannibals** sweatshirt, and he looked so cute except for one little thing: He's been outside in the sun so much his face has run together into one big *freckle*. I asked his dad when he'd be coming home, and he laughed like a lunatic and said, "Wally who?" The *least* he could do is send Wally some sunblock.

Actually, when I'm being totally honest with myself, I have to admit that Wally and I were never a true match. The other day I took this quiz in the latest issue of *Teen Scene* to find out what type of person I am and the kind of boy with whom I'm most compatible. It's *amazing* how much you can discover about yourself when you write things down on paper.

Favorite Foods: Corn dogs and miniature marshmallows.

Favorite Color: Blue. So's Campbell's. Wally's is green.

Favorite Music: Sousa and Little Tina.

Favorite Class: Current Events.

Favorite Books: The Bible and *SHORT BUT SWEET: The Little Tina Story*.

Favorite Movies: *Star Wars, Episode 17: Return of the Ghostly Peril* and *Love Story*, not the new one with the two guys, but the original, with the pretty, dark-haired girl with all the teeth.

Favorite Leisure Activities: Nipping off split ends, reading.

Pet Peeves: Negative people who always complain and take themselves too seriously, and people who smoke cigarettes or drink or take drugs. *Yuk!*

Most Embarrassing Moment: The time I was modeling swimsuits at Macy's and glanced down while I was waving—and my deodorant had dried all white and cakey!

Biggest Inspirations: God and Little Tina.

Then you were supposed to write a personal ad describing yourself, like the kind people put on the Net or in newspapers, which I'd never do, not only because my mother would kill me, but also because you never know what you'll get. Shelby met this guy on the Internet and he sounded so perfect, but when they finally met, he turned out to be completely different! How was she supposed to know what "vertically challenged" meant? He should've *told* her he was a midget!

But I wrote out the ad as a learning experience: "Blonde and beautiful, sunny and fun. Loves dancing, laughter, life," et cetera. Then you wrote a description of your ideal mate: "Wanted: Strong, handsome blond with sunny personality. Must love laughter, dancing, sports," et cetera—and it sounded *exactly* like Campbell!

I was so excited I called him up to tell him but he and his dad were having a big fight about his dad owning stock in tobacco companies. Campbell told his dad that he'd rather dig ditches than have *blood money* pay for his college tuition, and his father said, "Fine, grab a shovel." I told Campbell that I admire his commitment very much, but it's not like what his dad does will make a bit of difference.

"As usual, you're missing the point!" Campbell said, then *we* started arguing. But it worked out fine. Which is one reason we're so perfect together; it's like he's the snarl and I'm the conditioner.

My mother and I just got into it again.

I was standing in my bedroom in front of the mirror, practicing my screaming for the audition.

"What's the matter, Tiff?" she asked from the doorway. "Did you just remember that you have to do the dishes?"

"Why can't Retardo—"

"Tiffany!" she barked.

"Well, can't he do them tonight? I'm busy!"

"He did them last night," she said.

"So? It's not going to kill him. Tomorrow's the audition!"

"Aren't you supposed to be rewriting your essay for Miss Jones?" she asked.

"I am!"

"You are? It looks like you're standing there screaming," she said.

"I'm *going* to, I mean. As soon as I've practiced."

My mother sat down on my bed. Which is never a good sign; it means we're going to have a big discussion. I didn't have time for a discussion right then. I had to work on my fear reactions!

I said, "Do you think I look more terrified like this, or like this, with my hands in the air?"

"Pretend you're looking at your last report card. That'll help," she said.

"There's no need to be sarcastic," I said. "I know you're not happy about the movie. But the people spoke and the board voted. This is a democracy."

"Not anymore. It's a studio audience."

"What's *that* supposed to mean?"

She sighed. "Honey, sit down for a minute. Please." She patted the bed, and I sat down beside her. "You know that I love you very much, don't you, Tiffany?"

"Yes," I said.

"Even when we disagree," she said.

"I know."

"And I realize that you're a young woman now, with a mind of your own. Seventeen years old . . . "

I could see where this was heading. The next thing I knew, she'd be getting all weepy and dragging out my baby pictures.

"That's right, Mom." I tried to speed things up. "But I'll always be your little girl." No soap.

"Tiffy, have I ever lied to you, or intentionally steered you wrong?"

"Well, no," I said. "Except when you bought me those bell-bottomed pants."

"Aside from that."

"They were really ugly."

"Listen to me, honey." She took my hand. "Sometimes I think you don't realize how important your education is."

"Mom, my GPA—"

"I'm not talking about grades, Tiff, or using them to get a job that pays a lot of money. I'm talking about knowledge," she said. "About expanding your mind and your horizons."

"I did great on my SATs," I pointed out.

"Yes, you did." She squeezed my hand. "And Daddy and I are so proud of you, honey. Just as proud as we can be. You're a very intelligent girl, and I believe that you're going to accomplish great things. But you've got to focus on what's important, Tiff. Take advantage of this time in your life to grow and explore and plan for the future."

"I've already got a plan," I said. "I'm going to be an actress. Though I think they're all called 'actors' now, which, in my opinion, is only right. I mean, I'm not one of these feminists—"

My mother sighed.

"—who thinks that all men are dogs, or wants to play professional football. But women should get paid just as much as men and be treated with the same respect. So *what* if I like to wear pretty clothes and makeup? You can still be feminine and be a woman."

Hint, hint. But she didn't get it.

She said, "I just hope you won't be too disappointed if this movie business doesn't work out."

"I'll *make* it work out! There wouldn't even be a movie if it weren't for me! Mr. Goldman said so himself. So I know I'll get a part, and even if it's small, I'll do my best and lots of people will see me; important people like directors and producers and agents, and one thing will lead to another."

"Maybe so," she said. "But what if it doesn't? I don't want to see you hurt, Tiffy."

"Don't worry." I gave her a big hug. "I'll be fine."

It's funny and kind of sad how, as time goes by, you kind of turn into the parent and your mother's like the child. It's funny how things switch around.

"Promise me you'll put your schoolwork first," she begged. "You've done so well until this year! What's happened to you, Tiff? You've changed so much. You don't even have the credits to graduate."

"Will you *please* stop worrying about that?" I said. "There's plenty of time before the school year ends."

Then my mother started crying—we're talking mood swings here—and going on about the mind being a terrible thing to waste; and how easy it is, in this day and age, to get sidetracked and seduced by false values, et cetera.

"Tiffy," she finally said, tears in her eyes, "do you understand what I'm trying to tell you?"

I gazed into that dear, familiar face, her love for me etched in lines of worry, her careworn cheeks as pale as milk, and said, "Mom, have you ever thought of using blusher?"

She hit the ceiling. But it got me thinking. At the audition tomorrow, when I start screaming, I should make sure the veins in my neck stick out.

Chapter Ten

I got the part! I didn't even have to try out!

The auditions were held in the gym after school, and the place was an absolute *zoo*. Half the town was there: students, parents, the school board, the city council, et cetera, hoping to get a part in the movie.

Unfortunately, Principal Brown had forgotten to reschedule the basketball game, so the Cubberly Cougars and their fans arrived and were milling around and shouting. Our team, including Campbell, who's the captain, looked embarrassed. He and the other team's captain got into an argument.

Then Principal Brown ran in and apologized for the mix-up, and the Cougars stomped out and got back on their bus, but their coach blew up and claimed we'd forfeited the game! Which was *totally* unfair.

Finally the audition got under way, and the one thing that was a *tiny* bit disappointing was that most of the parts were already taken—by professional actors who aren't even teenagers! Mr. Goldman introduced them, and they stood up and waved, and they had to be at *least* in their twenties!

Mr. Goldman explained that due to labor laws, et cetera, they have to use union members or the movie couldn't get made. But he said that all we students will be in the movie: in "long shots" in the hallways, and in the prom scene and the dream sequence, when the pool looks like it's full of blood and hundreds of floating bodies.

He added that they won't be using real blood; they'll color the water, and when the filming is done, they'll drain and resurface the pool—for *free*!

Then Ms. Stuart stepped up to the microphone and said she had a *very* exciting announcement: The star of the movie will be *Little Tina*!

Everybody went crazy and looked around, trying to see her, but Ms. Stuart explained that Little Tina was taping her talk show in New York and would be flying in next week!

People were cheering and clapping and going nuts, but I took a moment to bow my head and give thanks to the Man Upstairs. Think about it: first Campbell, then the movie, now Little Tina!

I pray that someday I can make God as happy as He's made me.

♥ ♥ ♥

Ms. Stuart said that, in the past few weeks, they'd been observing all the students and had decided to use several of us to fill small speaking roles—and *The Girls and I will play the cheerleaders who get turned into cannibal vampires!*

The Girls and I jumped up, we were screaming and hugging one another. Then somebody said that wasn't *fair*; why should the stupid cheerleaders get the *real* parts when everybody else will just be seen opening their lockers or floating facedown in the pool?

Some people even agreed! I couldn't believe it!

One thing I want to say right now: I am *sick* and *tired* of this negative attitude toward cheerleaders. Some people, like my mother, think we're just a joke. I'll never forget the look on her face when I told her, in ninth grade, that I'd made the Pep Squad. She looked like she'd swallowed something nasty that was coming back up! Is it *my* fault that the cheerleaders in her high school were a bunch of mean snobs who pushed her out of the locker room into the hallway in her underwear?

Believe me, being a cheerleader isn't easy. In the old days, all you had to do was be peppy and pretty and have firm thighs. Those uniforms are short! But now you must be a superb athlete as well. The Girls and I rehearse for *hours*. Our routines combine tumbling, juggling, acrobatics, and dance. We could get into the *circus* with some of these stunts, yet we *still* have to put up with kids making fun of us and parents who complain that our routines are too sexy!

People don't realize that if it weren't for us, the fans would just sit in the stands like lumps and our teams would not be cheered on to victory.

But ever since cheerleading was recognized as an official sport, people are taking it a *lot* more seriously. So I just want to take this opportunity to say a special thank-you to the Olympic Committee.

Luckily, Ms. Stuart stuck up for us, noting that cheerleaders are *experienced performers*, and describing all of the legwork I'd done to make *Scream Bloody Murder* a reality. Then she asked me to stand up and take a bow.

I can't describe the incredible feeling that swept over me . . . not just because people were applauding and screaming; but because I knew, deep inside, where it counts, that I had made this dream come true.

Hardly anyone booed.

Then Ms. Stuart and Mr. Goldman answered questions from the audience. They explained that extras who have speaking parts will be paid the standard wage, and that most of the "shooting" on campus will take only a few days, although they'll probably come back for "retakes," et cetera. Mimi Durning asked if any frogs or animals would be killed in the film, but Ms. Stuart said no, just teenagers.

Then Bradley Knight got up on behalf of the Black Students' Union and said that it was *outrageous* that they were making this racist film on a public school campus; just *wait* until the ACLU and NAACP found out, but nobody knew what he was talking about. It turned out he was referring to the cannibals angle, but Ms. Stuart quickly explained that the cannibal vampires aren't *pygmies*; they're *white*. Then Bradley said that wasn't fair either; there should be black vampires, too. Ms. Stuart revealed that one of the main vampires will be played by *Keanu Mogatu*, the center for the *New York Knicks*, and everybody, including Bradley, applauded loudly.

Speaking of pygmies, I'm worried about Wally. Apparently a staff member misinterpreted his **Cannibals** sweatshirt and got mad and chased Wally into the jungle. I have *got* to call his dad tonight and see if they ever found him.

Then Ms. Stuart and Mr. Goldman had everybody line up at long tables to fill out cards with their height, weight, Social Security numbers, et cetera. The people staffing the tables were part of the movie's "technical crew," all wearing black T-shirts with *Scream Bloody Murder* in dripping red letters. Mr. Goldman announced that everybody in the movie would receive one of these valuable collector's items—for *free*!

The Girls and I asked Ms. Stuart if she wanted to hear us scream, but she said no, she'd heard us at a pep rally. She said that the writers are still "polishing" the script and that she'll get back to us as soon as it's ready. In the meantime, she added, don't gain any weight. She explained that people tend to photograph heavier than they really are and she looked right at Shelby while she said it. Too bad Shelby can't get a slight case of the pukes. Just kidding. Bulimia is nothing to joke about, and I'm getting a little concerned about Ashley, even though she *insists* she's not *trying* to throw up, she's just got a sensitive stomach.

I wanted to ask Ms. Stuart about my part, and if I'm the head of the Cannibal Vampire Cheerleaders like I am in real life. But she was yukking it up with the school board members, so I went outside and spotted Mr. Goldman talking to Campbell, who was still in his uniform and dribbling a basketball the whole time Mr. Goldman was talking.

I hurried over to see what was happening, but just as I got there, Mr. Goldman handed Campbell his card and said, "Think about it." Then he went back inside the gym.

"What was *that* all about?" I queried.

"He wants me to be in the movie," Campbell said, shooting a basket, then passing to his teammate, Tim. "He wants me to play the captain of the basketball team."

"That's fabulous!" I hugged him. "You heard what they said; only a few of us will get speaking parts."

"No, I didn't hear them. I was outside," Campbell said, shooting another basket.

"You're going to do it, aren't you?"

"No."

I couldn't believe it! How could Campbell act so impossibly *childish* just because his stupid game got canceled?

Well, not stupid. You know what I mean.

I said, "For heaven's sake, Campbell. It's only one game!"

"As usual, Tiff, you're missing the point," he said. "You can't see the forest for the artificial trees."

"What's *that* supposed to mean? Will you please stop dribbling?"

"Tiff, get a grip," he said. "Who *are* these people? How do you even know they're for real? They come in here with this cheesy movie—"

"It's *not* cheesy!" I said. "And they *are* for real! The chamber of commerce checked them out!"

He said, "The chamber of commerce would start a stampede downtown if they thought it would attract publicity."

"Campbell," I said, "I'm very disappointed in you. How can you be so selfish?"

He actually laughed at me! Then he said, "T-Rex, it's just a movie."

Just a movie? How could he even use those two words in the same sentence?

"'Just a movie'?" I said. "What about *Titanic*, or *Gone With the Wind*? I suppose those are 'just movies,' too."

"*Scream Bloody Murder* is no classic," he said. "It's just another dead teenager flick, with plenty of naked bodies."

I was shocked. How could Campbell be so *crude*?

I said, "It may not seem like a big deal to you, Mr. I'm-too-good-to-be-a-model, Mr. Seen-and-done-it-all-in-LA. But try looking at things from *my* point of view. My dream is coming true! And this is only the beginning! I'm not going to play vampires forever!"

"Why not?" He passed to Tim. "They never die."

"I'm going to do important movies!" I said. "About things that really matter! Like life! And death! And dysfunctional families! You can't start at the *top*, you know; you have to start at the bottom and work your way up!"

"Oh, Tiffy," Campbell sighed. "You just don't get it."

To my horror, I suddenly *burst* into tears. They flooded down my cheeks. It was *awful*.

"I know what people think of me!" I cried. "They think I'm stuck-up and conceited and phony and don't care about anyone! But that's not true! I *know* that millions of people in the world are starving! I could cry my eyes out, but what good would that do?"

I *was* crying my eyes out. Campbell and Tim just stood there, staring.

"I want to help people!" I wept. "And make this world a better place! With liberty and justice for all! But you can't do *anything* if you're just a normal person, living out a tiny little unimportant life! You've got to be *big* to accomplish something!"

I thought Campbell, of all people, would understand. I collapsed in sobs. He put his arms around me.

"Tiffy, I'm so sorry," he said. "I didn't mean to make you cry."

"This is great," I blubbered. "Now I'm acting like a baby, where everyone can see me!" I pressed my face against his chest to hide my embarrassment. Also, my nose was running.

"It's all right, Tiff." Campbell held me close. "You've been under a terrible strain. Worrying about Wally and this movie stuff. I'm sorry, Tiff. I didn't mean to hurt your feelings. It's just that sometimes it seems like— I don't know—like you're under a spell and can't wake up."

"Then why don't you kiss me?" I cried.

Tenderly, so tenderly, Campbell kissed my forehead, and then each tear-streaked cheek. I'm not that into sex, but this is ridiculous. Why doesn't he ever kiss me on the *lips*? Could it be that Campbell respects me too much? Or could it possibly—a terrible thought crossed my mind—could it possibly be my *breath*? Even though I brush and floss and use mouthwash?

Just to make sure, I coughed into my hand, but all I could smell was Crest.

Campbell offered to take me home, but I told him I had to be alone for a while. I needed time by myself, to reflect and think, and to absorb the many changes that were taking place in both my personal and professional life.

Things were happening so fast. *Too* fast.

Chapter Eleven

I was just reading Little Tina's second autobiography, covering the past three years, age seventeen to twenty. It's hard to believe somebody that young— *good grief!* When will my brother stop *drumming*?

It's hard to believe somebody that young could have so many accomplishments in her life, starting with those famous toilet paper commercials when she was three, then soap operas, country music, movies, books, sportswear—not to mention her own TV talk show. A nice one, too, with no punching or screaming. Even the president of our country has been on it!

She's also got stuff in there like recipes for her favorite snacks, Weiner Boats with Cheese and Chocolate Haystacks; her thoughts about important issues facing teens today, like sex and drugs and implants; and lots of health and beauty tips. For example: If you've been sobbing, take two used tea bags—

Now my mother's screaming at my brother. How on

earth does she expect me to concentrate and do my homework with all this *noise*? This family is driving me insane!

Family is also very important to Little Tina, as is God, who's her best friend, so we have a *lot* in common. In fact, I was just arguing with Campbell about God. I'd called him up to say isn't it great that Little Tina is going to be in our movie, and to try to talk him into taking the part of the basketball captain. Most people would *kill* to have a real part, and here's Campbell acting like, Who cares, so what?

I said, "Can't you see God *wants* you to do it?"

"God wants me to be in a slasher film?" he said.

"It's *not* a slasher film!" I retorted. "It's a comedy!"

"What could be funnier than dead bodies?" he said.

Sometimes I think Campbell just likes to argue. He was really ticking me off, but I concealed it.

"Campbell, this movie is the opportunity of a lifetime!" I said. "Who do you *think* made it happen?"

"You?"

"Well, sort of," I admitted. "But I couldn't have done it without the Man Upstairs."

"Your grandpa's on the roof again?"

"That's not funny!" I said. "I won't even *talk* to you if you're going to act like that!"

He sighed. "I'm sorry I'm being so crabby, Tiff. I'm having some trouble with this math."

One thing I admire about Campbell: Not only is he handsome and a fabulous athlete, but he's also a very serious student. It's amazing, when you think of it, how much we have in common.

"What I was *trying* to say," I continued, "is that you should feel blessed by this opportunity He's giving you."

"Mr. Goldman?"

"God!" I said, but suddenly I was filled with dread. "You *do* believe in God, don't you, Campbell?"

"Not really. It seems so unlikely," he said.

My heart sank. How could I even *think* of marrying a man who doesn't share my faith? What about our children? They *have* to go to Sunday school! I loved Sunday school when I was little. We sang and drew pictures and drank pink punch. Nowadays I can't always make it to church, but I know that wherever I am, God is with me.

"How could there *not* be a God?" I said. "Otherwise, where did everything come from? The world and all the birds and stuff?"

"That's a long story, Tiff," he said. "And I've really got to get this homework done."

"Let me ask you one question," I said. "When you have a basketball game, don't you pray to God to help you win?"

"No."

"You *don't*?" I said. "Why not?"

"I'm sure God has more important things to do," he said. "Like wiping out child abuse and famine, for example."

"That's just the point!" I said. "He can do it all! He's *everywhere*, like Santa Claus on Christmas Eve."

There was a slight pause. I could hear Campbell breathing.

He said, "You don't believe in Santa, do you, Tiff?"

"That's it," I said. "End of conversation. But I really feel sorry for you, Campbell, I really do. You must be so empty inside."

I hung up the phone and said a quick prayer for Campbell. Then I remembered I should pray for Wally, too. It turns out that he never went back to his school! He's been spotted running around in the jungle, with paint on his face and his hair all crazy, wearing a *loin-cloth* and his **Cannibals** sweatshirt!

According to his dad, Wally's joined some native tribe and may even have taken a native *wife*! What on earth can Wally be thinking? He's *way* too immature to get married. And you'd think he'd at *least* have the decency to tell me! We haven't even officially broken up!

I blame myself—and Shelby—for this. We should never have told him about Campbell.

When Wally's dad told me the news, I said that I would be willing to go on worldwide television and *plead* with Wally to listen to reason and act normal and return to his school.

I'd tell Wally that I know what it's like to feel hopeless, and like you don't have the strength to carry on, but that every cloud has a silver lining, and it's always darkest before the storm.

Wally's dad said that was a very nice offer, but there was one tiny problem: There's no television reception in the jungle.

Poor Wally. What a *nightmare* this must be for him. He loves to watch TV.

I noticed that on the cover of Little Tina's book, there are the words "As Told To" and somebody's name in tiny little letters you can barely read. I was thinking of asking Miss Jones to help me turn this video journal into a book, but then we'd have to split the profits, and besides, she never takes me seriously. When I told her my plan to turn this into a best-seller, she said, "That's very interesting, Tiff. But shouldn't you be working on your essay?" She'd made lots of little red marks on the pages so I could make improvements when I rewrote it.

Like I've got the time! Besides, I want my writing to sound fresh and real, like this journal. Just me, talking. They could call it *Talking With Tiff.* Or *Tiffany Talks.* And put on the cover: "In Her Own Words," with a really nice picture of me, and more inside. And the book will be full of my thoughts and feelings and be a real inspiration to all the teens who feel like "befores" in a world of makeovers.

So maybe I should say something about my health and beauty regime.

No matter how beautiful you already are, *nothing* is more important than the glow of good health. *Do:* Eat plenty of vegetables and fruit and protein. Take a daily multi-vitamin with minerals. Get plenty of sleep. And drink at least eight glasses of water a day. I know, that's a lot! Sometimes I feel like I'm floating away!

Don't, and I mean *don't,* drink alcohol. Think about it: That stuff literally poisons your brain!

Do not smoke cigarettes. This can't be emphasized enough. Smoking stinks up your breath, makes your face gray and wrinkly, and causes serious health problems too numerous to mention. In all honesty, I can truthfully say that I'd rather have a live *frog* in my mouth than a lit Camel.

Do *not* get a tan. Too much sun not only can cause cancer, but it also makes people's skin look like beef jerky.

Do not, under any circumstances, take illegal drugs of any kind: uppers, downers, pot, the works. They screw up your brain and *ruin* your body. It's like trying to run your car on Coke—the kind you drink—instead of gasoline. Your body is a temple; why treat it like a motel? Remember: Your body is where you'll be living for the rest of your life!

Last, but never least, *Get plenty of exercise*. Not only will you look great, you'll feel great, too. Every day before school I: s-t-r-e-t-c-h (keep those muscles limber!), do five hundred jumping jacks, lift weights for upper body strength, and practice my cartwheels and splits, et cetera. Not to mention all the exercise I get leading cheers.

It's funny, in a way, how some people see cheerleaders, like we're just a bunch of jockette bubbleheads. All of The Girls and I are on the Principal's Honor Roll (I might be slipping a tiny bit lately) and will be going on to college. This prejudice is even worse if you're a natural blonde like me, or even an unnatural blonde like Shelby.

Which reminds me: I have *got* to get her more motivated. Lately, she just stands there during games like, "Yay, so what." Does she want to be a cheerleader or not? Ashley yells her little heart out and Barbie and Kendall give it everything they've got. Which, unfortunately, is not quite enough. Don't get me wrong, they're great girls, but we're not talking personality plus. And I always get the name wrong when I give them helpful hints, like, "Barbie, go all the way down on your splits."

"I'm not Barbie, I'm Kendall."

It's irritating.

But what makes our cheerleading squad so successful is that we put aside all our little differences and work together as a team. For example, when that fight broke out yesterday after Donny fumbled the ball on the twenty-yard line, The Girls and I started singing the National Anthem. Almost everybody stopped what they were doing and joined us, which gave the refs a chance to drag the nitwits off the field. It's amazing how immature people can be. You just want to say, "Come on, you guys! Will you *please* try to act like adults?"

Too bad some people think winning is so important. We won! Fourteen to seven!

Chapter Twelve

I can't believe I'm saying this and I never thought I would, but Little Tina is *not* a very nice person.

We were all so excited before she showed up on the set today to have publicity pictures taken. Everybody, except Campbell, was waiting outside the gym, including *hundreds* of junior high school kids waving Little Tina Fan Club signs.

The tech crew made everybody stand behind barricades so they couldn't get too close, except for Jason Wittington, who plays her boyfriend in the movie, and The Girls and I, who play her gang.

For the record, I would like to state that Campbell is every bit as good-looking as Jason, whose skin, in real life, is not too great. Why Campbell refused to play the basketball captain, Jason's best friend in the movie, I'll *never* understand.

Then the longest limousine I've ever seen pulled up and people started screaming and flipping out.

"Here she is!" Mr. Goldman shouted, and he ran over and opened the door—and this *tiny little person* got out. I mean, I always knew Little Tina was small, but she's practically—I hate to say it—a *dwarf*. She looks so much *bigger* on TV!

She was wearing a cheerleading outfit just like ours and carrying red-and-black pompoms. But I couldn't *believe* it: She was smoking a cigarette! In her book, it says she *never* smokes!

Then a bunch of fans ran over and tried to touch her and somehow knocked the cigarette out of her mouth, and one of the pompoms caught on fire.

Principal Brown rushed over and stomped it out and told Little Tina that Hiram Johnson High is a tobacco-free zone.

"What makes you think it's tobacco?" she snapped.

So things weren't off to a very smooth start. I agree that smoking is a very bad habit, but the *least* Principal Brown could've done was to welcome her to our campus. For heaven's sake, she's a *star*, not a student! It's not like he can put her in detention!

Unfortunately, the incident seemed to affect Little Tina's mood, and she wouldn't even *look* at me and The Girls when Ms. Stuart introduced us.

Then she asked, "Which one is Jaycee?" which is

the name of my character, the leader of the cheer-leader gang. When Mr. Goldman pointed me out, she got this expression on her face, like I was a plate of *dog* food or something, and said, "No, her look isn't right."

Excuse me, please? My *look* isn't right? This was clearly a case of professional jealousy because, in all modesty, I'm *just* as beautiful as Little Tina, and at *least* six inches taller.

To my horror, Mr. Goldman seemed to agree with Little Tina and started saying maybe Jaycee should be played by one of the other Girls, possibly Shelby! I thought for sure The Girls would say no, it's got to be Tiffany. But it turned out that they *all* wanted the part, except for Ashley, who hates it when we argue, and got an instant migraine.

Luckily, Ms. Stuart took my side and explained that Shelby was a little too porky—she put it more nicely— to play Jaycee, and the decision had been made and it was *final*. If Little Tina didn't like it, Ms. Stuart said, she could talk to her agent. In the meantime, could we *please* get the damn pictures taken?

But there's one thing I've got to say for Little Tina: She is a true professional. She put aside her differences, wrapped her arms around us, and posed for all those pictures with a big smile on her face.

It's just kind of disillusioning. Little Tina seems so *nice* on TV! On her talk show she always gets tears in her eyes when somebody tells her a sad story.

I know that a big star like her is under a lot of pressure, and the microscope of constant public scrutiny. But if it weren't for us fans, she wouldn't be *anybody*. When *I'm* famous, I'll never be one of those stars who refuses to give autographs and complains that they can't get any privacy. Come on, people! It's called *show* business, not *no*-show business. If you want privacy, drive a cab or be a teacher!

Speaking of teachers, while all of this was going on, my mother and a bunch of other teachers were *picketing* in front of the school, carrying signs that said, "MAKE GRADES, NOT MOVIES," "EDUCATION, NOT ENTERTAINMENT," and "STUDENT BODIES, NOT DEAD BODIES."

It was really embarrassing.

Mr. Goldman told me not to feel bad and explained that they were filming the picketing, which will be shown as funny "outtakes" at the end of the movie.

You'd think the teachers would recognize that this is a great opportunity for us students, but it's like they think we should be learning something every single second! One reason Principal Brown acted like such a *butthead* today is because the superintendent and the school board overruled him and decided to have minimum days while the camera crew is on campus. Most of the movie will be shot in a studio, so it's not like our school will be "disrupted" forever. Why can't he *see* that?

The mood around the dinner table tonight was *tense*. What's happened to my mother's sense of humor? When I told her the picketing had been filmed for funny bloopers, I thought she was going to have a *stroke*.

She said, "You really don't get the point, do you, Tiffany?"

What a joke. *She's* the one who's overreacting.

But I decided to be mature and just smooth things over, so I told her the linguini was superb.

Then my father tapped his glass with a spoon and said that he and my mother had important news.

I almost choked. I was afraid he was going to say that they were having a *baby*! But it was much worse than that. He and my mother are planning to move.

"Move?" I exclaimed. "You've got to be *kidding*! Where?"

I thought that Retardo would be upset, too, but he just said, "Huh!" and kept shoveling in the food.

"Yes," my mother said. "We've decided to escape the rat race and move to the country."

I was stunned. "*What* country?"

"The country," my father said. "Somewhere up on the north coast, where the air is clean and the living is easy."

He and my mother actually smiled at each other and reached across the table and held hands!

"We've *always* lived here! What's wrong with this place?" I asked.

"This used to be a lovely town," my father admitted. "But it's gotten so crowded and noisy."

"What do you mean, noisy?" I said.

My mother complained that, no matter where she goes, she can always hear freeway traffic.

"What are you *talking* about?" I demanded.

"That sound," my father said. "Don't you hear it, Tiffy?"

Well, sure, now that they'd mentioned it. But couldn't they just pretend it was the ocean? I mean, here they were, ruining my entire *life*, and I hadn't even gotten a *vote*!

Sobs burst from my throat. "Well, I'm not going!" I cried. "You just don't want me to be in the movie! But it's not going to work! I'll run away! I'll stay with The Girls! I'll live with Campbell! Retardo doesn't have any friends—"

"Tiffany!" barked my mother.

"—so he doesn't care, but how can you *do* this to me?"

Reeling from this devastating blow, despair and panic overwhelmed me. We were more than halfway through senior year! There wasn't *time* to go to a new school and get popular! Not to mention how this would affect my studies.

I stopped pounding my head on the table so I could hear what my father was saying.

He was explaining that I should calm down, that they wouldn't be moving until *after* I'd graduated, in June. Anyway, he said, I'd soon be going off to college.

I couldn't believe it. They seemed so happy! As if they couldn't *wait* for me to go!

I was *dying* inside, but of course they didn't notice: They were too busy planning their Tiffany-free future. Even my brother is glad they're moving! That just shows what a moron he is!

My parents said they're going to buy a big house on the coast and turn it into—get this—a combination *bed-and-breakfast inn/nursing home*. As if the tourists won't notice that half of the "guests" are ninety years old and in wheelchairs!

"Won't Grandpa be pleased?" my father said. "He

loves the beach! And it's time for the generations to come together. Old people are being marginalized and warehoused," et cetera.

I know he's been under a terrible strain, coming up with all these cutting-edge inventions, not to mention managing the enormous volume of business that 1-800-YOR-MAMA generates. Let's face it: Those calls are depressing. No wonder he's cracking up.

But my mother should know that this move is a *terrible* idea. For heaven's sake, she's a teacher, not a genius! You'd think she'd have more sense!

Sadly, it appears that losing the battle against *Scream Bloody Murder* has pushed her right over the edge.

Chapter Thirteen

Campbell pulled out my chair so I could sit down, and my heart practically melted, right there in the restaurant. Wally never remembered to do stuff like that. Poor Wally. If he ever comes back, he'll probably eat with his hands or try to order grilled ants.

Naturally, Campbell ordered the vegetarian plate and I chose rack of baby lamb, although I wish they hadn't put that word "baby" on the menu. You'd think I'd ordered a live toddler from the disappointed look Campbell gave me.

But I didn't say anything to spoil the moment. I wanted the evening to be perfect, a new beginning for Campbell and me.

Maybe I'm only imagining things, but it feels like Campbell and I are drifting apart, like ships on a stormy sea. He's in such an impossible mood lately—and he seems to be blaming *me*.

Was it *my* fault that the swim team couldn't

practice today because the movie crew had to use the pool? How strong and sleek he looked in his wet Speedo when the assistant director made him get out.

For Pete's sake, the filming won't last forever! It's just taking a little longer than we expected, due to technical difficulties.

First, Jason Wittington came down with that terrible cold sore on his lip, so they had to shoot—meaning film—around him. But it turned out he must've been contagious *before* it erupted because Little Tina got a big cold sore, too. The makeup crew tried to cover it up with pancake, but it looked like she had a poisonous *yam* under her nose!

The writers worked the cold sore into the script, like it was some kind of cannibal vampire virus, but Little Tina said— Well, I won't say what she said. I would never use words like that in my book.

And then there were the problems with the school board scene.

The *real* board, playing the school board in the movie, was supposed to be discussing whether to allow the filming of a "slasher" movie on the school grounds, kind of a movie-within-a-movie type of thing. The "AD"—assistant director—told the board members they could ad-lib their dialogue, meaning improvise, so it would sound spontaneous and natural.

My part was the biggest. It was even written down. I was supposed to say all the stuff I'd actually said the night the school board approved the filming of *SBM* on campus.

But the board members ruined *everything*! Every darn one of them tried to hog the whole scene, interrupting each other, making speeches, et cetera.

They wouldn't even let me *talk*!

Then Principal Brown barged in, shouting that there was a gang fight outside, but everybody thought he was just trying to disrupt the filming again, until the SWAT team and the ambulance arrived.

I had no idea that making a movie was so *emotionally*, as well as physically, draining.

The plan now is to wrap up all the shooting during spring break, while everybody's on vacation.

I know that we have to get back to real life eventually, but I'll sure be sad to see the movie crew go. It's like we're one big happy family!

I think that's the problem with Campbell and me. I've been so busy with the movie that I haven't been giving him enough attention. Boys think the whole world revolves around *them*.

I guess I thought Campbell was more mature.

"Earth to Tiff," he was saying. "You're not listening to me."

"Of course I am," I replied as the waitress served our salads. "I was just thinking how handsome you look."

It was true. I could look at Campbell forever. And not just because he's so good-looking, but because his face is so honest and strong. It's a face you could trust with all of your secrets. If I *had* any secrets—which, to be honest, I don't, but if I did—I wouldn't hesitate to tell him.

"I was asking if you'd heard from any of the colleges you've applied to," he said.

"Not yet."

"Me neither," he said. "It's too early, I guess."

I didn't mention that things have been so *hectic* that I haven't had a chance to complete the applications. Campbell would have a fit. He takes school so seriously! He's almost as bad as Miss Jones. In class today, she was ranting and raving about this new toilet paper called Canned Classics, or Classics in the Can, that has great works of literature printed right on the rolls, famous old stuff like *Moby Dick*. You'd think she'd just be glad that people are reading!

"How's your salad, Tiff?" Campbell asked.

112

"Yummy," I answered.

He started saying how much he wants to be a good doctor and promote healthy lifestyles, et cetera, but there was a bean sprout stuck in his front teeth and I kept wondering, should I tell him or not? Some people get offended when you tell them stuff like that, but personally, I would *want* to know if something green was hanging out of my mouth. Luckily, it disappeared while he was talking.

One thing I've always been thankful for: My teeth are so perfect and straight. Ashley's had her braces practically since she was born, and believe me, it's hard to keep them clean. She always covers her mouth when she laughs. Could *that* be one reason she's not eating?

Sometimes I think I should become a psychiatrist and help people understand their problems.

" . . . so I told him he doesn't have to pay for my tuition. I'll get a basketball scholarship and apply for loans."

Apparently Campbell was discussing his father again, and their disagreement over the tobacco company stocks. It's wonderful that Campbell has so many principles, but sometimes people take things to extremes. For example, my mother thinks it's *disgusting* that in *SBM* we're doing what's called "product placement." That means a company pays the movie company money to have the characters eat a certain brand of potato chips, in this case, Lay's; or cereal, Frosted Flakes; or to drink a certain beverage, in this case, Coca-Cola.

"It's like everything's an ad for something else!" she said this morning. "I mean, look at you, in your Nike shoes and your Guess jeans and your *Scream Bloody Murder* T-shirt!"

I tried to explain to her that everybody does it: in movies, TV shows, professional sports, et cetera. She snapped, "That doesn't make it right."

"No," I said, "but it doesn't make it wrong."

Sometimes you just can't reason with her.

Personally, it doesn't bother me at all; you just have to hold the Coke can so the logo shows. Unfortunately, Shelby can't seem to grasp this difficult concept. We've had to do take after take after *take* because she keeps turning her can the wrong way or holding the bag of potato chips upside down.

It's been grueling.

"Don't you think so, Tiff?" Campbell asked.

"Absolutely."

In the "Boyfriend Beat" column of *Teen Scene* magazine, they always advise: "When in doubt, agree."

And, generally speaking, I *do* agree with Campbell, but he always wants to talk about injustice and problems, while I prefer to look on the bright side of life. For heaven's sake, we're kids! We've got our whole lives to be miserable! How am I supposed to enjoy my dinner if he keeps talking about pollution and lung disease?

"By the way," I said, tactfully changing the subject. "Are you going to buy a videophone?"

"No, I'm not," he answered stubbornly. "I've already told you a million times."

He *insists* on using the old-fashioned type, where you can't even see who you're talking to. Sometimes that's okay, like when my father has to change his voice to take the 1-800-YOR-MAMA calls. It would be too confusing if the people saw him. But there's no excuse for Campbell not to get a videophone. He'd even look good in the bathroom!

I said, "Don't you want to see me when we're talking?"

"Not really. I don't forget what you look like," he said.

"But then we'd be in total communication," I explained.

Which, of course, started him having a big fit about

privacy and technology, et cetera, et cetera. What an old fuddy-duddy he can be! He never wears the cell phone I gave him for his birthday. He's not even hooked up to the Internet!

"I'm glad we're finally spending some time together," Campbell said. "I feel like I've hardly seen you lately, with this dumb movie going on."

"I wish you wouldn't call it dumb," I said.

"Tiff, please," he said. "I couldn't believe that stupid scene in the library where the freshman got eaten. And now they've dumped all that blood in the pool."

"*Fake* blood," I pointed out. "It's not like they slaughtered a whale in there or something."

An important point, but I was sorry I'd brought it up right then because the waitress had brought our dinners and Campbell was staring at my plate like someone had *tortured* my baby lamb. Why did they have to use that word "rack" on the menu?

Sometimes it seems like the two of us are so different that it will be a *miracle* if we stay together. Then I think of all the things we share: Our love of sports and music and dancing. Our scholastic aptitude and sensitivity. How good we look in formal wear. Which reminded me: "Campbell, I've been meaning to ask you to be my escort at Macy's Spring Fling Fashion Show," I said. "They're looking for some handsome guys."

I thought he would be flattered. But instead, he got this *look* on his face.

"Tiff," he sighed, "I know we're friends, but do I *have* to?"

This is the thing I can't understand about Campbell. You'd think he'd be glad that he's so good-looking that Macy's would want him to model their clothes! Plus he'd make some really good money.

"I thought you'd be pleased," I said, a little hurt.

"You know how I feel about modeling," he answered.

"This isn't about modeling; it's about *us*," I said. "Are we a couple or aren't we?"

"A couple of what?" Campbell said.

I've never put all of my feelings into words, but Campbell *must* get the picture by now! Do I have to spell everything *o-u-t*?

Hot tears sprang to my eyes. I busied myself buttering some French bread.

Campbell took my hand. "I'm sorry, Tiff," he said. "I'll do it, if it's so important. But sometimes it seems like . . ." He glanced down at his plate.

"Seems like what?" I persisted, when he faltered.

"Well, like you think I'm an accessory or something," he said.

"An accessory?" I repeated. "What do you mean?"

He said it was hard to put into words, but something about me thinking that he's like a *handbag*; just something that looks good, to wear on my arm, and that I don't really get that he's an actual *person*.

Which is absolute unmitigated *crap*. But I didn't say that; I refuse to be crude. Choking on tears and my French bread, I replied, "If you don't understand, I can't explain it."

The waitress came back and asked if everything was okay.

"Fine, thanks," Campbell answered, gently waving her away. Then he said, "I think I know why you're so upset, Tiffy."

Finally. "You do?"

"Yes," he said. "I know how worried you are about Wally. Have they found him yet?"

What *is* it with boys? How could somebody as smart as Campbell be so *dense*?

"No!" I gasped, struggling for control.

"Don't worry; they will. Wally's going to be fine. He'll be back home before you know it," he said.

Suddenly it all seemed hopeless. Campbell has too many principles to be my boyfriend! He obviously still thought of me as "Wally's girl" and was just holding down the fort until Wally returned!

But how could I tell Campbell the truth: that

whether Wally ever comes back from the jungle or not—which I hope he does—we're *through*? Campbell would think I'm unfaithful and shallow. His image of me would be shattered.

". . . you're such an intelligent person," he was saying. "But you get all caught up in this phony stuff—"

"Phony stuff?" I couldn't believe my ears. "Like what?"

"Oh, the movie, and these stupid fashion shows. I mean, look around you, Tiff. There are problems in the world."

"You're telling me," I said. "Yesterday on the *Larry Singer Show*, they had these Siamese twins. And the really sad part is, they can't stand each other—"

Campbell exploded. "How can you watch that guy? That's the worst show on the air!"

I was shocked by his tone of voice, and more than a little irritated.

"I realize there are problems in the world," I said. "I just don't see why we have to *talk* about them all the time."

"Because things won't change until we face the facts and quit hiding our heads in the sand," he said. "It's called denial."

"Yes, I know what it's called, Mr. Smartypants," I said.

"That's what I can't understand," he continued. "You're so smart, Tiffy. There's a real person inside you. But for some strange reason, you'd rather be a fake. I mean, not to hurt your feelings—"

"It's a little late for that!" I snapped.

"—you think all of this stupid stuff is so important; like how people look and being a star. What *difference* does it make if you're famous or not? This is real life, Tiff, not television."

"Too bad," I said, "or I could turn off the sound."

Talk about not being on the same page! We weren't even in the same *script*! I'd pictured this evening turning out so differently: the two of us holding hands across a candlelit table, soft music playing in the background, Campbell whispering those three little words that mean so much: "Let's go steady." Not that we're not going steady already, but it would make it more official.

I said, "I didn't realize you found me so disgusting, Campbell."

"You know I don't," he said. "But it's like you're choosing not to use your brain. Why do you always have to be so relentlessly superficial?"

I could've socked him. "What do you mean, 'relentlessly'?" I said.

"Come on, T-Rex!" he said. "You don't let up! Going

on and on about all this stuff. Who *cares* about Little Tina's cold sore?"

"Two billion people, that's who!" I said. "You're just mad because you couldn't use the pool!"

"Who wants to swim around in blood?" he practically shouted.

"It's *fake* blood!" I explained. "It's a comedy!"

"It's stupid!"

"No, it isn't! That just happens to be your opinion!" I said. "And another thing. What's this T-Rex stuff? What's *that* supposed to mean?"

Campbell looked embarrassed. He said, "You really don't know?"

"No, I don't! Tell me!" I glared at him until he did.

"Tyrannosaurus rex," he quietly admitted. "The biggest meat-eater of them all."

Our waitress came back. "Would you care for some dessert?" she asked. "We have a wonderful cheese-cake—"

"Well, that just takes the cake!" I stood up and grabbed my coat. "I had no idea that's how you saw me, Campbell; as some kind of giant *lizard*."

"I don't," he stammered. "I'm sorry, Tiff. I just meant you have a strong personality."

Our waitress left.

"I can't believe this," I said, tears filling my eyes.

"You think you know somebody, but you don't. I thought we were such good friends!"

"We *are* good friends." Campbell took my hand. "I'm really sorry, Tiff. I shouldn't have talked to you like that. I didn't mean to lose my temper."

"It's too late for apologies now," I said, struggling to regain my composure. "And after we do the fashion show, Campbell, I never want to see you again."

"Tiffany, please," he said. "I didn't mean to hurt your feelings. I was just trying to be honest. That's what friends do. And I want you to be honest with me, too. So tell me I'm an idiot. Tell me I'm a dope. But please, sit down and finish your dinner."

His eyes pleaded with me. My heart melted again. The cheesecake was really good.

So the evening ended on a happy note. But later, after Campbell had taken me home, the scene in the restaurant haunted me, replaying in my mind again and again.

Was it true, like Campbell said, that I'm just a big phony who doesn't really notice anybody but herself and wants life to be like TV, with everybody watching and everything all beautiful and glittery?

No. If that were true, this book would have only the good parts, not the parts where people are calling me a jerk.

Chapter Fourteen

All *heck* has broken loose. Something *horrible* has happened.

Four days ago, TV talk-show host Larry Singer was EATEN by his studio audience.

I wouldn't believe it myself, if I hadn't seen the film clips. We watched them on the news that night while we ate dinner.

Larry's show is—was—always broadcast live because it gave him such an edge in the ratings. You never knew when a family would start strangling each other, or taking off their clothes, or rushing into the audience to attack them.

But something went terribly, terribly wrong that day.

It all started innocently enough. Larry was interviewing a middle-aged married couple who claimed to be cannibals. The studio audience got *all* worked up. They were screaming at the couple and punching their fists into the air, chanting: *"Lar-ry! Lar-ry!"* They were practically going *insane!* Which was what they usually did, so that didn't seem too strange.

Then it looked like they were giving Larry a standing ovation but—and here's where things got really tragic—they actually attacked and *ate* him!

No matter how many times I see that footage in slow motion, I *still* cannot believe my eyes.

Naturally, my mother started ranting and raving that shows like Larry's are ruining our country, making young people rude and callous, et cetera. She actually tried to turn off the news, but my brother said—and for once I agreed with him—"No, I want to see it!"

On every channel, an anchorman or woman was saying: "In a bizarre twist today, TV talk-show host Larry Singer . . . ," and then they'd show the clip again: Larry shaking his head and smiling sadly into the camera, like he couldn't understand why anyone would want to be a cannibal, then looking kind of puzzled as the audience rushed toward him.

"For God's sake!" my mother shouted, leaving the table. "You'd think they'd have the decency not to show it!"

Later, all the regular shows got canceled and on every network there were big discussions: Should the footage of Larry being eaten have been shown? Was it news or exploitation? How could an entire studio audience be prosecuted for murder? Would their lawyers use the "mob mentality" defense? et cetera, et cetera.

And of course it brought up all the tired old arguments about whether a former president of the United States like Larry should be allowed to host a talk show.

For heaven's sake, it's a free country! What are ex-presidents *supposed* to do, open a shoe store or something?

One thing that was really sad: Larry always ended his shows by looking into the camera and saying, "Ciao"—which is Italian for "good-bye"—"baby!" The next day the newspaper headlines read: "CHOW BABY!" Which, in my opinion, was completely tasteless.

But the absolutely *worst* thing about all this—besides Larry being dead, of course—is the negative attention and bad publicity that's been focused on *Scream Bloody Murder.*

News crews have been all over our school, interviewing the principal, the teachers, the janitors, et cetera, asking, "What's this business about a cannibal movie? Was a freshman really eaten in your school library?" et cetera.

As if we'd somehow caused this awful thing to happen!

When the assistant director was interviewed on

Channel 7, he explained that cannibalism is a *very* small part of *Scream Bloody Murder*; that the movie is mostly about vampires, and, as everyone knows, they just drink people's blood, their victims live forever, et cetera.

But that didn't seem to help. The school board has been *flooded* with phone calls demanding an end to filming on campus.

It's been a nightmare.

At first I was hoping that the whole thing would blow over, so we could achieve closure and the healing process would begin. But it's like Larry's death has taken on a life of its own. Hardly anyone—including The Girls, I'm sorry to say—wears their **Cannibals** shirts to school anymore, except for the losers and the gang members. Principal Brown is even talking about *banning* the **Cannibal** and *Scream Bloody Murder* shirts from Hiram Johnson High!

Can he just *do* that? What is this, Russia?!

Today the AD called all the cast and crew members together, except for Little Tina, who had flown to Washington, D.C., to sing at Larry's funeral. The AD explained that Little Tina won't be back. The rest of her scenes will be filmed at the studio.

Although it was an honor to work with Little Tina, she could really be a pain in the drain sometimes, throwing a fit whenever she didn't get her way, insisting on being shot from a certain angle so that *my* face was always turned away from the camera, et cetera.

Perhaps, like Campbell says, I've been living in a dreamworld. But I honestly had *no idea* that such a big star could act so small.

After a moment of silence in Larry's memory, the AD explained that they were going to speed things up and finish the filming on campus as soon as possible.

Which was disappointing. For one thing, I'll hate to see the movie people go; they make school so exciting! And for another, I was hoping to meet the movie's *real* director, Mr. Cosmo Sloan, who is considered the father of slasher comedies. Unfortunately, he's on location somewhere, filming the sequel to *SBM*.

If only Ms. Stuart and Mr. Goldman were still around. The AD and I have never really clicked. He doesn't seem to get that if it weren't for *me*, this movie wouldn't even be happening!

From what Ms. Stuart had said, I thought my role would be a whole lot bigger. But unfortunately, Little Tina was so jealous of me that she *insisted* that my part be shrunk. I've ended up doing lots of cartwheels and cheers and just saying stuff like, "Wow, that's cool!" or "You're kidding!"

In fact, they actually made me stand in a *ditch* so Little Tina would look taller!

I wish I could talk to Campbell about all this, but I know he'd say, "I told you so!" He even thinks Larry's death is funny!

I said, "I can't believe you'd say that, Campbell. I thought you were a vegetarian and *against* capital punishment."

"Yes, except for talk-show hosts," he replied.

Has the whole world gone *insane*?

Usually I'm not a superstitious person, but it seems like Larry's ghost is haunting the movie. *Nothing* is going right.

Today we were supposed to shoot the locker room scene, where The Girls and I change into our cheerleader uniforms just before the big game against our arch rivals.

The next thing you know, there's Principal Brown—doesn't he have a *job* anymore?—making a big scene about us being in our underwear, and saying that wasn't in the script he approved.

The AD admitted that a few changes had been

made, but per their agreement, there would be no nudity on campus, and that underwear's the same as bathing suits.

"No, it isn't!" Principal Brown insisted, and he had a big old honking *fit* until they rewrote the scene to have us horsing around in the pool in our swimsuits, then being in such a hurry to get dressed that we put our uniforms on *over* our wet bikinis! It didn't make any sense!

But the AD seemed very happy with the pool scene, although I hadn't realized that the water was so *red*. I thought it might be better if I didn't get in, just sat on the diving board and waved et cetera, but the makeup man assured me that the water wouldn't stain my hair. Which, unfortunately, wasn't true, but it finally rinsed out. That's *all* I need—a blood-colored head!

The other bad thing that happened is that Ashley has dropped out of the movie.

I should've seen it coming; she's been acting so strange. But the other day it all came to a head. In scene after scene, she could *not* get her lines right. Then we were filming some funny outtakes and Ashley was supposed to "fluff" her lines; in other words, make mistakes on purpose. But she couldn't! Time after time, she kept getting them *right*! The AD's AD totally blew up at her, and she collapsed in tears and had to be carried off the set.

Nothing bothers Shelby, even when it should, and Barbie and Kendall are so easygoing. But Ashley is supersensitive to stuff, and the excitement of the movie has taken its toll. She isn't even coming to school anymore; she's on independent study. Her doctor says that what she has is like the *opposite* of claustrophobia. She's gone into her bedroom closet and won't come out

In the meantime, the show must go on. So they cast, of *all* people, Mimi Durning, who'd just—what a nut—*completely shaved her head*, in some kind of protest against fur or leather shoes or something. She handed out these stupid little pamphlets on the set, and she didn't even spell "America" right; she spelled it with a "K." What an idiot!

Then, as if things weren't bad enough, the AD got the *brilliant* idea that it would be a great effect if *all* of the cannibal vampire cheerleaders shaved their heads and burned their hair in the bonfire at the big game rally!

As you know by now, I take my career very seriously, but I spoke for all of The Girls when I said that shaving my head was absolutely *out* of the question. So instead they put Mimi in an Ashley-type wig and said that nobody will notice the difference.

I realize that it's necessary to make sacrifices for my career, but it's like my hair is part of me, and I'm proud that I stood up for my beliefs. But now I'm worried that I might get a reputation for being "difficult," which could negatively impact my future success.

I wish I could discuss my fears with Campbell, but he practically splits his sides laughing when I tell him what's happening behind the scenes.

And my mother and I seldom talk these days.

This morning she said, "Tiffany, I feel like I hardly know you anymore. If somebody came up behind me with a garrote, I think you'd just stand there."

"I don't know," I said. "What's a garrote?"

She wouldn't even tell me! She thought I was being sarcastic!

Can't she see that *she's* the one who's changed, not me? I feel like I could wake up some night and find her driving a wooden stake into my heart!

It seems like my mother is blurring the lines between the movie and reality.

Chapter Fifteen

My life has exploded like a shimmering balloon in the hands of an evil child; my hopes and dreams shattered on the rocks of reality. I've been crying so hard my eyes are puffed shut. I could barely see to turn on the videocamera just now.

But there's no use putting it off any longer.

Scream Bloody Murder has been canceled.

Even as I hear myself saying those words, I still cannot believe that it's true.

But it is—and my life has become a nightmare from which I cannot wake up.

I heard the rumors when I got to school this morning.

"Did you hear the news?" everybody asked me. "The movie's been canceled!"

At first I thought they were talking about *Bobby Becomes a Man*, the hygiene movie they show to the freshmen, which a group of concerned parents has been trying to ban.

"No!" everyone said. "*Scream Bloody Murder*! They're not going to finish it! It's canceled!"

Not being a person to jump to conclusions, I assumed that there must be some logical explanation. Perhaps all of the filming had been completed ahead of schedule.

But we hadn't even shot the muddy-football-field scene yet, where The Girls and I wrestle the rival team's cheerleaders.

None of it made any sense. My heart began to hammer in my chest.

Fighting a rising tide of panic, I went directly to Principal Brown's office. At first he wouldn't even *look* at me, but I just stood there, glaring, until he got off the phone.

"Tiffany," he sighed. "Can I help you?"

"Is it true?" I demanded. "Has *Scream Bloody Murder* been canceled?"

Then he uttered the word that will forever be branded in my memory.

"Yes."

I burst into tears. "How could you *do* that?"

I accused him of trying to *ruin* our school spirit,

pointing out that he'd done everything in his power to stop and then undermine the movie, which would've put Hiram Johnson and our town on the map. "How could one man," I asked, "be so heartless, so *selfish*?"

Wracked with sobs, I paused to catch my breath.

Principal Brown stated that it wasn't his fault. He explained that there was a "conflict of interest" between the Pepsi company, which had supplied the boys' football uniforms and owned the vending machine concession on campus, and the Coca-Cola company, which had paid the movie company a great deal of money for product placement in *SBM*.

"Not only that," he added grimly, "both of the soft drink companies are threatening to sue the school board and the district for damages and breach of contract."

Or something like that. I didn't get all of it because right around then I went into *shock*. My body was *numb*. I couldn't even *talk*.

Staggering out of his office, I saw the undeniable proof that what he had been telling me was true. By the Snak Shak, rival soft drink employees were arguing in their gang colors: red and blue for Pepsi, red and white for Coke.

I wanted to cry out, "Can't we all just get along? Can't we work together for the red, white, and blue?"

But my tongue had withered in my mouth.

I stumbled to the parking lot, found my car, and drove home. I have no idea how; I was practically *unconscious*. Hours later, when I finally came to, I was lying on the family room floor, watching an old episode of *I Love Lucy*.

That was days ago. At first I tried to go back to school, but it's like everybody is blaming *me* for what happened with the movie!

Is it *my* fault that the pool got permanently stained so that it looks like the swim team is practicing in blood? The movie people promised that the color would come off, but now they say they *aren't* going to fix it, and on top of that *they're* suing Hiram Johnson, too!

Even The Girls—except for Ashley, who's still in her closet—are actually embarrassed to be seen with me! I always knew that Shelby thought that *she* should be the leader of The Girls, not me. But I never realized that Barbie and Kendall were such fair-weather friends. This afternoon I called Kendall and she said, "I can't talk now, Tiff. I have to practice the piano."

She *never* practices the piano! Who does she think she's kidding?!

♥ ♥ ♥

Through all of this pain and humiliation, Campbell has been wonderful and a tower of strength. He hasn't even mentioned the pool still being red. He keeps encouraging me to see the humor—*what* humor?—in the situation, and telling me that everything will work out for the best, et cetera.

The other day he took me for a drive to the coast to take my mind off my problems. We had lunch in a tiny little town called Elk, in a restaurant overlooking the ocean. The sky and the sea were a breathtaking blue, and way in the distance, we could see whales spouting. Later, we walked along the beach holding hands, and a playful seal skimmed across the waves beside us.

Campbell pressed a sand dollar into my hand. "Don't spend this all in one place," he said, grinning.

My eyes filled with tears. I felt so happy and peaceful.

But driving home we passed through the town of Manchester, and I was suddenly enveloped in a fog bank of gloom. That's where my parents are going to open their combination bed-and-breakfast/nursing home. They've bought a big old farmhouse with lots of land and chicken coops that can be converted into guest rooms. They plan to call it the Home Sweet

Home Home. Or the Home Sweet Home House. Something like that.

What are they thinking? There's *nothing* in Manchester, just the ocean and a post office and a grocery store. You can't buy clothes or furniture or *anything*. Don't get me wrong; it's a nice place to visit, but how are my parents going to *live* there?

Miss Jones dropped by after school today to bring me my homework. She told me not to let all this movie business get me down.

"So what if it didn't work out?" she said. "It's better to travel than to arrive," et cetera.

I know she means well, but doesn't she realize that *Scream Bloody Murder* could've been my big break? Lots of important people would've seen me in the movie—directors and producers who would've recognized my talent and known that I'm not just another pretty face.

She said, "Now that the movie's over, Tiff, you can buckle down and catch up on your schoolwork. You've got to take that makeup test, and you still haven't handed in your essay," et cetera.

I tried to look interested in what she was saying, but my head felt like a bowl of confetti. I just can't seem to *concentrate* lately. Dean Schmitz keeps leaving messages on the answering machine saying that I've got to come in right away and discuss my credits for graduation.

But that all seems so meaningless now. So futile.

Since I've been at home, I've watched lots of TV: game shows, comedies, *The Best of Larry Singer*, et cetera. But I *never* watch the news. It is *so* depressing. Baseball players striking, gas prices rising, that meteorite hitting the Netherlands. All those people, all those tulips—*gone*, in the blink of an eye.

And I absolutely *will not* look at a newspaper. For one thing, they always print a bunch of stuff that's not true—like what they wrote about *SBM* and why it got canceled. "An anonymous Hiram Johnson spokesman described the movie production as a 'fiasco' and referred to cheerleader Tiffany Spratt as 'precious and precocious—but ruthless.'"

Ruthless! *Me!*

On top of *that*, the newspapers ran a really ugly picture of me with my mouth hanging open, like someone had just socked me in the stomach. And they took everything I said out of context, so I ended up sounding like a total *nut*!

Now I understand why some stars refuse to have anything to do with the media.

♥ ♥ ♥

But sometimes good things come out of tragedy. And I have to say that, during this difficult time, my family has really been there for me. Even my brother. He doesn't say much, but it was cute today how he gave me the last snack pack of Doritos. That spoke volumes.

And my father is still my biggest fan—showering me with compliments, bringing me flowers, and playing Sorry with me for hours, to take my mind off things.

My mother keeps saying I should go back to school.

"You can't just lie around and watch TV," she says. "You've got to get back on the horse that threw you."

I know she's right, but she doesn't understand what it's like to be a social *outcast*, to walk through the halls of my own school and know that people are laughing behind my back!

I got furious at her the day the movie deal collapsed, when she tried to tell me she was sorry it had happened.

"No, you're not!" I said. "You're *glad* it was canceled! You never wanted it to happen! You tried to stop the whole thing!"

"Of course I'm not glad it was canceled," she said. "I could never be happy when you're hurt."

"Yes, you are!" I shouted. "You thought the whole thing was stupid! You said so a million times!"

"That doesn't mean I think you're stupid, honey." She tried to hug me, but I wouldn't let her.

"Yes, it does!" I screamed. "You think I'm stupid! You hate me!"

I ran upstairs and slammed and locked my bedroom door. She knocked for a long time, but I wouldn't answer.

It wasn't fair of me to take it out on her like that, but I'd never felt so bad in my whole life! In one single day I went from being Miss Popularity to Miss *Piranha*, or however you say that word that means Miss "Reject of the Universe."

That night I couldn't sleep. I kept looking in the mirror to see if I'd turned into someone else and mistakenly ended up with *her* life. But the face looking back from the mirror was mine, all puffy and red from crying.

"Oh, my God," my mother said, looking up from the newspaper tonight. "I don't believe this."

"What is it?" asked my father. We were all in the kitchen. He was making dinner, my brother was doing his homework, and I was circling programs I didn't want to miss in the latest issue of *TV Guide*.

She continued, "The medical examiner's office announced today that autopsy tests on former president and talk-show host Larry Singer have been concluded. According to the coroner's report, Mr. Singer wasn't human at all, but was in fact a rare strain of flesh-eating bacteria.'"

"It says that? Where?" My brother actually got up to look.

I know she was trying to cheer me up, but my mother can be so crude.

"That's not funny," I told my mother. "You shouldn't make jokes about Larry."

"I'm sorry, honey. Hey, did you see this editorial?"

The editorial, inexplicably entitled "I'm ready for my closeup, Mr. DeMille," said that it was time to "bury" *Scream Bloody Murder;* and for the school board to stop blaming everybody else, "including the young lady whose only crime was in trying to make her dreams come true."

"Hey, Tiff, that's you!" my brother said.

The editorial stated that it was "ludicrous" for the school board to blame Principal Brown for the pending lawsuits, since *he* was the one who had advised them *against* permitting the movie to be filmed on campus.

"It's about time someone talked sense," my father said. "Doesn't that make you feel better, Tiffy?"

"No!" I said. "Do you think the kids at school are going to read that editorial or care what it says? They're still going to think I'm a big fat *loser*!"

I ran upstairs and threw myself on my bed, the tears pouring out of me in torrents. A gentle hand began to stroke my back. My mother was sitting on the bed beside me.

"Tiffany," she said, "please listen to me."

"I can't go back to school!" I moaned. "They all hate me!"

"No, they don't," she said. "Besides, it's not your fault that the movie folded. Those legal problems have nothing to do with you."

"I know," I groaned, "but if it wasn't for me, none of this bad stuff would've happened!"

"Look at it this way, Tiff," she said. "None of the good stuff would've happened, either. None of the excitement, none of the fun. And just think—you got to meet Little Tina."

"She wasn't very nice!" I sobbed.

"No, she wasn't," agreed my mother. "But like the editorial said, life is one big classroom."

"But I wanted to be in the *movies*!" I wept. "I wanted to be on TV!"

"Forgive me, sweetie," my mother said gently, "but I still don't understand why that's so important."

"Because you're famous!" I cried. "People care what you do! You're not just some tiny little *ant*! You're important! And you never get ugly and old! You always look good in reruns! Forever! I don't want to get old, Mom! I don't want to just die and people won't even know I existed!"

"I know," she murmured. "It's a lousy system. But it's something we all have to face."

"But I don't want to be like everybody else!" I said. "Don't you understand, Mom? I want to be different! I want to be someone *special*!"

"Oh, honey bunny, you are," she whispered, gathering me into her arms.

Chapter Sixteen

I never thought I'd say this, but my mother was right. Everything has turned out fine!

I'm back at school again and the kids are being really nice to me. Even Mimi Durning! Yesterday I was brushing my hair in the girls' bathroom and she came in and started putting glitter on her head, and her eyes met mine in the mirror.

Mimi told me that she owed me an apology.

"An apology? What do you mean?" I said.

She explained that she'd never actually thought of me as a real person until the day the movie deal collapsed, and she saw me leaving the school parking lot and driving down the street in reverse.

"You always seemed so perfect," she said, "and like you didn't have any feelings. Maybe I was just jealous of you."

"That's okay. I don't blame you," I said.

We even gave each other a *hug*!

And The Girls and I are together again, even Ashley, who's back at school and has gained ten pounds and looks a whole lot better!

Sometimes I still feel a little mad at The Girls for turning against me when I needed them most and dropping me like a hot potato. But I realize now that we *all* have our faults, and that we shouldn't let a small misunderstanding stand in our way. I mean, we've practically been friends forever! We'll probably be bridesmaids at each other's weddings!

I really feel like I've learned a *lot* from this experience and my mistakes.

The *best* thing that's happened is that all the legal problems have been solved! The cola companies decided *not* to sue our school because it didn't look too good for public relations. And the movie company has announced that it's not going to sue us either! They're going to complete *Scream Bloody Murder* after all, so it isn't a total loss!

Unfortunately, all the scenes filmed at Hiram Johnson have been dumped and are being reshot at a high school in LA. So there goes my big break. *But*, and was this ever a load off my mind, *SBM*'s insurance company paid to have the swimming pool resurfaced!

So it's better than ever now, thanks to me!

♥ ♥ ♥

Anyway, who could feel depressed in the spring? The days are so sunny and warm, the birds are singing, and all the trees and flowers are in bloom. It makes me feel so hopeful for the future. Like my mom said, the end of *SBM* wasn't the end of the world. I still have Campbell and my friends and my modeling career. There'll be plenty of other big breaks down the road. For Pete's sake, I'm only seventeen!

And I realize now, after everything I've been through, that there's more to life than fame and success. *Much* more. I'm even thinking of putting off college for a while and joining the Peace Corps.

When I told that to Campbell, he was very impressed. But that's not exactly why I said it. I really believe that when a person has been blessed with money, looks, intelligence, et cetera, they owe it to God to give something back to life.

Campbell says I seem much more considerate and mature.

Another good thing that came out of all the bad stuff that happened is that I really appreciate my parents now, and how they try to make the world a better place. My dad comes up with all these great ideas and inventions, and my mother has devoted herself to teaching, although she plans to quit when they move to the coast and open their Home Sweet Home House. House Home. Whatever it is. I can never remember. Which may or may not pan out, I don't know. But we all have our dreams, no matter how dumb they are, and they deserve a chance to blossom and grow.

One thing I *do* feel guilty about: I've been so wrapped up in myself and my own problems that I haven't gotten around to calling Wally's dad and finding out how poor Wally's doing. The last I heard, he'd been found in the jungle and returned to his school. In a cage!

Doesn't Wally understand that the sooner he gets with the program and cooperates, the sooner he'll be able to come home? I wish there were some way I could explain it to him. Maybe I'll write him a letter tonight, if I'm not too exhausted.

But first—on with the show!

If there is *anything* more exciting than Macy's Spring Fling Fashion Show, I don't know what it is! It is truly the highlight of the season.

This afternoon, as I was putting the finishing touches on my makeup in the dressing room, I bowed my head and said a special thank-you to God. I mean, *think* about it. What a privilege it is to get to wear beautiful clothes and walk out onto the stage and down the runway with my darling Campbell, in front of newspaper photographers and an adoring crowd, when half of the world is naked and starving.

It makes me feel so humble and so blessed.

That settles it. I am *definitely* going into the Peace Corps.

I wonder if you can choose where they send you.

Campbell has never looked more handsome than he did tonight, and I could tell that The Girls were really envying me. But they tried to be good sports about it, even Shelby, who was stuck with that lunkhead Bryan, who fell off his skateboard on the way to Macy's and knocked out his two front teeth.

The other reason The Girls might have been feeling a tiny bit jealous was because at the end of the show *I* was the one who'd get to wear the June Bride gown while *they* had to be my bridesmaids. It wasn't *my* idea. Mr. Margo said he picked me and Campbell because we are the ideal couple.

It's true. And not just because we look so good together. We're soul mates, through and through. During the entire *SBM* ordeal, when all my hopes and dreams were crumbling, Campbell stood by my side and never faltered, or tried to act like he didn't know me. He never even threw the pool in my face!

I just hope that I can always be as good a friend to Campbell as he has been to me. And someday, if it pleases God, his wife.

Mr. Margo has a motto that is tattooed on my brain: "The model's final effort must be to conceal the effort that it takes to be a model."

In other words, being pretty, professional, and poised isn't enough. There's a *lot* more to modeling than just smiling and strutting your stuff!

Not only do you have to know how to walk and turn and pause, showing the clothes to full advantage, and *not* blink your eyes, so you'll look intense, but you must also be able to undress *very quickly* and get into a new outfit and back onstage without looking like the clothes were thrown on you from a speeding car.

Plus, try to "suck in your gut and tuck up your butt" for two hours! That's our other motto.

Believe me, it's not easy!

But I love the work. There is something so rewarding about hearing all those cameras clicking, and the way the audience oooohs and aaaaahs when you make your entrance in a fabulous dress. Plus, when it comes to making money, it sure beats babysitting!

♥ ♥ ♥

The first part of the show went smoothly as Campbell and I took a "Cruise to Alaska," dressed for church in our "Sunday Best," toured Europe in our "Around the World" coordinates, and decided to "Paint the Town Red" in our matching "Grad Night Party" ensembles. Which reminds me: I have *got* to call Dean Schmitz! He's absolutely *swamped* the answering machine with messages and has even started calling my parents.

In between our appearances, The Girls and their escorts modeled casual apparel: "Sun 'N' Surf," "Tennis, Anyone?" et cetera. I know The Girls were disappointed that they didn't get to wear more dress-up stuff, but I told them that they still looked great.

Then finally it was time to prepare for my big entrance, the show's grand finale: the "June Bride" scene.

As Mr. Margo assisted me with the rows of tiny genuine pearl buttons, the clouds of veil, and the shimmering white train, a thousand butterflies fluttered in my stomach. I was thinking, this is how it will be in real life someday, for Campbell and me, with The Girls, my best friends, there beside me, sharing that golden moment.

"Tiffany, you look so beautiful!" The Girls gasped, even Shelby. Grateful tears sparkled in my eyes.

Campbell saw me backstage, just before we made our entrance, and the look on his face made me cry some more.

"Tiffany, you look like an angel!" he breathed. "You'll make some lucky man so happy someday."

"So will you," I stammered. "You look so handsome, Campbell." He looked *fantastic* in his snow-white tux accented with a single red carnation. "Too bad you can't dress like that all the time."

He laughed—I guess he thought I was joking—then he took my hands and said, "Seriously, Tiff, you're a beautiful person. Inside and out. Some man will be proud to call you his wife."

I wanted to shout, "It's *you*, Campbell," but my eyes said everything that needed saying. He kissed me on the cheek and wished me luck, then took his place behind the curtain.

I'm *already* the luckiest girl in the world, I was thinking, struggling to control my emotions. But suddenly The Girls were crowding around me—and *they* were all crying, too!

"Tiffany," Barbie wept, "we just want to tell you—

"—how much we all love you!" Kendall cried.

"And how sorry we are for feeling jealous of you sometimes!" Ashley sobbed.

"And for all the mean things we've said behind your back!" Shelby sniveled.

"Darling, don't cry." I gently touched her cheek. "You'll make your mascara all smeary."

"Do you forgive us, Tiffy?" they asked.

"Of course I do," I said.

And as I said the words, I knew that they were true. Through all of my trials and tribulations, I have become a bigger, better person—forged in the flames of foolish pride and smelted in the coals of redemption.

"Everyone makes mistakes, Girls. Even me," I admitted. "Can all of you forgive me, too?"

Then we were blubbering and hugging each other until Mr. Margo came over and said, "Please, girls, you're stressing the satin."

But as I took my place, I couldn't help wondering, *What* mean things had they said behind my back?

But there wasn't time to dwell on that; my future was unfolding like a rainbow-colored ribbon. The tape recorder began to play "The Wedding March." Campbell walked onstage and took his place beside the altar.

Then The Girls, my bridesmaids, slowly filed onstage, looking *adorable* in their matching teal-blue dresses, in *spite* of all Shelby's reservations. She'd said the dresses were the color of her grandmother's veins.

The moment had arrived: It was time for my big entrance. Mr. Margo gave me the signal and I moved onto the stage. "Small smile," he hissed. "No teeth." *Step, pause*. The audience gasped when they saw me and broke into wild applause.

Step, pause. Step, pause. I was trembling all over, imagining that this was only a rehearsal for what would be the happiest day of my life. *Step, pause. Step, pause.* I could barely see where I was going. Spotlights, flashbulbs, and tears flooded my eyes. I was blinded by—I guess you'd call it joy.

But as Campbell moved forward to greet me at the altar, something in the front row of the audience caught my eye; someone who made my brain reel with *shock*, as I recognized the tufts of reddish hair, the face that had tanned into one big *freckle*, the cheeks etched with scars in a primitive design.

"Tiffany!" he cried. He wasn't even wearing a *shirt*.

"WALLY!"

I pitched forward, blacking out.

Chapter Seventeen

I haven't left the house or been back to school all week. And not just because I landed on my nose when I fainted. Thank *heaven* my black eyes are finally fading.

How can I *ever* face Wally again? After everything he's been through, how can I tell him that it's over, that Campbell and I are together now and practically *engaged*? Not that I want us to get married right away; I think we should graduate from college first and get our careers going.

But I feel so *guilty* when I think of poor Wally, hacking through the jungle to get back to me, the memory of our love his only hope . . .

I'm afraid this will break his heart.

The first few days after the FASHION SHOW FROM HELL, Wally kept calling and coming by the house, but I wouldn't answer the phone or the door and finally, he went away. I haven't even talked to Campbell or The Girls. I feel like I'm living all alone, on the planet of Tiffany.

Why on *earth* did Wally carve those weird designs into his face? I almost had a heart attack, he looked so strange, like some kind of clown in a scary movie. Couldn't he have surprised me when the fashion show was *over*? Snapshots from a nightmare haunt my brain: me, lying on the floor; people staring down, shocked; Mr. Psycho-Clown shouting my name; the "Wedding March" playing . . .

My parents urged me to go back to school right away. They told me that the swelling was hardly noticeable.

"Your face looks fine," they said, but they were just being kind. I looked like I had a pair of panty hose pulled over my head.

Don't they realize how *cruel* kids can be to anyone who looks the slightest bit different, even if the person can't help it?

I just want you to know, God, that I *get the message*, and that I'm sorry for every mean thing I've ever done.

But I *still* don't see why Mimi wants to go around looking like Mrs. Potato Head.

This morning my mother came into my room and insisted that I go to school.

"Tiffany," she said, "you're so far behind in your studies. Besides, don't you want to spend time with your friends before everyone leaves for college?" et cetera.

I turned from the mirror, where I'd been gazing at my face. The swelling had subsided and the skin around my eyes wasn't purple anymore. I was ready to face the world—and Wally—again.

"All right, Mother," I said. She looked so happy and relieved!

Which reminds me: Wasn't Mother's Day last week? Do they sell belated Mother's Day cards?

My father gave me a big hug and kiss when I came down for breakfast, and as I drove to school, I knew that I had made the right decision. It was time to face the music, smell the coffee, bite the bullet.

Which is something I hope all of my future readers will remember if anything like this ever happens to you. No matter where you go, you can't hide from yourself. So you might as well put a big smile on your face and say, "Here I am, Life! Take your best shot!"

It was heartwarming, how glad everyone was to see me. Even Dean Schmitz waved and called my name.

But I didn't have time to talk to him right then. As I stood at my locker, getting out my books, I saw Wally walking down the hall toward me.

Silently, I prayed for strength. The *last* thing I wanted to do was hurt poor Wally, after everything he'd been through already.

"Hey, Tiff!"

At least he was wearing a shirt, but his hair was still tangled and crazy. He kissed me on the cheek.

"Hello, Wally," I said, smiling fondly at him. "It's good to see you at school again."

"Yeah," he said. "My dad decided to let me come back so I can graduate with my class and everything."

"That's nice," I managed, but my ears were ringing. Then I realized it was the bell for first period.

"You look good," Wally said. "I missed you, Tiff."

"I missed you, too," I stammered, then added, "I heard you got married."

He smiled, embarrassed. "It was more like going steady," he said. "Things are different in the jungle."

"I'll bet. Anyway, that's okay," I said. "You must've been so lonely."

"I was," he said, "but your letters really helped."

The scars on his cheeks were twin spirals, and it looked like there was a tiny *chicken* carved on his chin. Poor Wally. Even if Campbell and I weren't going steady, there's no way Wally and I could've gotten back together. Too much has happened; we've grown apart. And Macy's would *never* have let him be my escort again.

"I'm sorry I scared you at the fashion show," he said.

"That's okay," I said. "You didn't mean to."

"And I'm sorry I haven't called you lately," he said.

I had to hide a smile. It was so ironic! Wally thought *he* hadn't been calling *me*, when *I* was the one who'd been avoiding *him*!

"It's just that—I don't know how to tell you this, Tiff," he said, "but I've fallen in love with someone else."

My smile stuck to my teeth. "I beg your pardon?" I said.

"I know this sounds crazy," he said, "but it was love at first sight, like I was seeing her for the very first time. Even though we've known each other since kindergarten. Do you know what I mean, Tiff?"

"Uh-huh," I managed.

"I didn't want to hurt your feelings," he said, "but I knew you'd want me to be honest, Tiff, 'cause that's the kind of person you are."

"Uh-huh," I said.

I'd carefully rehearsed the speech I'd planned to

give to Wally. Now here he was, giving it to *me*! We would always be good friends, he said. He hadn't meant to let me down. But so much had happened; we were different people now. Did I think that I could ever forgive him? et cetera.

"Of course I can, Wally," I calmly replied, while a voice inside me screamed, *You're not breaking up with ME, you twit; I'm breaking up with YOU!*

But what was the point of hurting Wally's feelings? I felt proud at how much I've changed and grown. The *old* Tiffany would've acted like a spoiled brat, but the new, improved Tiffany was mature.

Besides, this made everything a whole lot easier.

"These things happen," I said. "Who's the lucky girl?"

"Mimi Durning."

"WHAT?" I said.

"I'm not kidding, Tiff," he said. "It's like magic or something, like there's some kind of electrical current between us."

He said a bunch more stuff—I could see his lips moving—but all I could think was: *Mimi Durning*? He's dumping me for Mrs. Potato Head?!

My mind reeled with shock, but I must've kept smiling, because Wally hugged me and said, "Thanks, Tiff. I knew you'd understand."

"Uh-huh," I answered.

"Well, we'd better get to class now," he said. "I'll see you later."

Then he pecked me on the cheek and was gone.

I stumbled through my morning classes in a daze. My teachers warned me about overdue assignments, my friends chattered happily about the fun we'd have in a few weeks at the Grad Night party. But their words were like tiny, whining insects in my ears. I brushed them away, lost in a world of my own.

Mimi Durning?! Why would *anyone*, even Wally, choose *her* instead of *me*?

Had his ordeal in the jungle driven him insane? Was he suffering from the effects of a tropical brain fever? Had he eaten some kind of hallucinogenic *frog*? I've read about stuff like that in *Reader's Digest.*

These were the thoughts tormenting my mind as I drifted in a haze from class to class.

At lunchtime Campbell caught up with me in the Senior Quad. I tried to smile and act normal, but he could tell that something was wrong.

"Tiff, what's the matter?" Campbell asked. "You look so strange."

"I think I'm allergic to egg salad," I said.

"I met Wally," Campbell said. "He's a really nice guy. You must be so glad to have him back."

"Yes," I said. I wasn't ready to go into all that. "Campbell, let's go for a ride after school. Someplace quiet where we can talk."

"Are you sure Wally won't mind?" Campbell said, and he winked.

"I'm positive," I answered.

"Great," he said. "I'll meet you in the parking lot after school."

He left for his next class, and I should have gone to mine, but school was the *last* thing on my mind. Suddenly I felt like I was sitting in the front row of the audience, watching a movie about my life. The camera had zoomed in for a close-up of Tiffany Spratt—and I didn't much like what I was seeing.

It was *ridiculous* of me to feel bad because Wally had dumped me! Was I that petty, that insecure? Did the whole world have to be in love with me? I didn't even want to be with Wally anymore!

I had to laugh at myself. And I'd thought I was so mature!

The problem was my pride, my silly, childish pride, preventing me from seeing that everything had worked out beautifully. I had everything (almost) that I wanted in the world. The *least* I could do was be happy for Wally, glad that he had come home safely and had found somebody to love him.

But *Mimi Durning*?!

Gosh darn it, I thought, you're doing it *again*! What *difference* does it make if Mimi's bald? My dad's almost bald and my mother still loves him! It's the cake underneath that counts, not the frosting! Campbell doesn't love me just because I'm beautiful. He loves me because I'm *me*! And I don't love *him* just because he's so good-looking. I love who he is *inside*, his spirit.

Sitting there, alone in the Senior Quad, I came to a deeper understanding of Life than I ever had before.

I felt like laughing and crying at the same time, like running through the streets, hugging everyone I saw. It was like an Academy Awards of the soul, but I knew I couldn't have done it alone; I owed it *all* to the Director upstairs.

"Thank you for loving me, God," I whispered, "even though I'm just a knucklehead."

We took Campbell's car and drove high into the hills, parking on a bluff overlooking the town, spread below us like a tiny toy village. All around us, springtime trailed her flowing green skirts, and I was reminded once again of what a blessing nature is, putting the puny world of man into perspective.

I wanted to share my spiritual breakthrough in the Quad with Campbell, but I sensed that words would be inadequate. So we sat in silence and listened to the wind and the birds.

"This is nice," Campbell commented, the breeze ruffling his hair like invisible, loving fingers.

"Campbell, there's something I have to tell you," I finally said.

"What is it, Tiff?" he asked.

"It's about the Peace Corps," I said. "I wasn't really serious about joining it, at first. I think I just said that to impress you."

"Why?"

"You know," I said. "Because you've always thought I'm so superficial."

Campbell's handsome face looked stricken. "Tiff, I'm sorry," he said. "I had no right to say that. You were just going through some changes, that's all."

"No, you were right," I admitted. "All I cared about was myself and my hair, and being a famous movie star."

"And cheerleading," Campbell added.

"But this year has been like a total learning experience for me," I said. "I've really changed and grown. Now I really *do* want to join the Peace Corps, and help others less fortunate than myself."

"That's wonderful, Tiff," Campbell said, smiling.

"Yes," I said. "I have so much to be grateful for."

"That's true," he agreed. "You must be so relieved that Wally's come home."

There was a slight pause while I assembled my thoughts.

"Well, sort of," I answered. "Wally and I aren't together anymore. He's going with somebody else now."

Campbell looked shocked. He said, "You're kidding. Who?"

"Mimi Durning."

"The girl with the head?"

"Yes," I said.

"Tiffany," Campbell said, "I'm so sorry."

"It's just one of those things," I said. "Wally and I have grown apart. There's too much blood under the bridge."

Campbell took my hand. "This must be so hard for you," he said. "I know how much you love him."

How can boys be so *thick*? Surely, Campbell must know by now that I love *him* as much as he loves *me*!

"We all have to grow up sometime," I said.

"Exactly," Campbell said. Then he looked so serious, as he gazed into the distance, that I wondered if he was thinking about the future. *Our* future.

"There's something I have to tell you, too, Tiff," he said. "In fact, I should've told you a long time ago, but I wasn't being honest. With myself or you."

Suddenly I knew what he was going to say and I got this *sickening* feeling in my stomach. The whole time Campbell and I had been together, he must've had a secret girlfriend in LA! So we *weren't* getting married! We weren't even going steady! I felt like I was going to *throw up*!

"I'm gay," Campbell said.

Who can explain the mysteries of the human brain or how the mind works when it's slammed to the mat? When I was a child, my father taught me Pig Latin.

"Ime-gay?" I said. "You mean 'Gime'? What's that?"

"Listen to me, Tiff. I'm gay."

"You're *WHAT*?"

Frozen in a timeless moment, we stared into each other's eyes.

I finally broke the spell that held us.

"But that's not fair!" I cried.

Campbell looked a little irked. "I know this will be hard to believe, Tiff," he said, "but I'm not doing it on purpose to bug you."

"Are you *sure*, Campbell?" I asked. "Maybe it's just a phase you're going through."

He shook his head. "I haven't been involved with anybody yet," he said. "It's just something I've always known, deep inside."

My mind struggled to make sense of the words it was hearing. How could someone as perfect and wonderful as Campbell turn out to be *gay*? Why was this happening to me? Had I done something awful in another life to deserve it? Like wiped out an entire civilization?

And if Campbell was gay, and seemed completely normal, that must mean there were other gay people at Hiram Johnson, who looked and acted like everybody else!

My mind was *spinning*. I was *so* confused.

" . . . which was why I never got heavy with you, Tiff," he was saying. "I didn't want to lead you on, or have you think that we could ever be more than friends."

"Oh, no," I said. "That never crossed my mind."

People at school would laugh right in my *face* when they found out I'd been going steady with a gay guy! Imagine what Shelby was going to say! How would I *ever* live this down?

"Your friendship has been an inspiration to me, Tiff," Campbell said. "You're not afraid to be yourself.

You always stand up for what you believe in, even when it's something kind of dumb—"

"Dumb?" I said. "Like what?"

"Well, like the movie."

"The movie wasn't dumb," I said.

He smiled and squeezed my hand. "What I'm trying to say, Tiff," he explained, "is that you give life everything you've got. You've helped me to be braver, too. Not that I'm ashamed of who I am. I just know that being gay makes life more complicated, because of the way some people react. But what difference does it make what other people think, if you know in your heart you're a good person, trying to do the very best you can?"

"Uh-huh," I said.

"Not that I need to shout it from the rooftops. My sexual orientation is my own business, not anybody else's."

"Exactly. I couldn't agree with you more," I said.

"I'm really sorry that I didn't tell you sooner, Tiff," he said. "I guess I couldn't even tell myself. And I was afraid that it would—I don't know, change the way you feel about me, or mean that we couldn't be friends. Now I know you're not that kind of person."

I wanted to scream: *That's what YOU think, bub!*

But the oddest thing happened then. I heard God's voice in my mind, plain as day, saying: "*Tiffany, the epiphany in the Senior Quad was only the beginning. Now it's up to you. Remember, it's the cake that counts, not the frosting.*"

How could I let God, or Campbell, down?

And in that moment my spirit broke free from all the fears that have ever shackled me. What *difference* does it make what other people think, as long as I always act with love and try to do what's right?

Everything was different then, and nothing had changed. Campbell was still Campbell. I was still me.

I said, "I love you even more, Campbell, now that I know who you truly are. And I really want to thank you for trusting and believing in me."

We held hands, smiling at each other through our tears.

"Friends forever," he said.

"Friends forever," I agreed. "But there's something I have to ask you, Campbell."

"Anything," he said gently.

"Will you still be my date for Grad Night?"

"Yes."

We laughed then and kissed each other, on the lips.

Chapter Eighteen

The most incredible, awful, *unbelievable* thing has happened.

Yesterday morning, Dean Schmitz called me into his office and told me that *I won't be graduating in June.*

"You don't have the necessary credits," he said.

At first, I thought he was joking, but the look on his face confirmed the terrible truth.

"There must be some kind of mix-up," I stammered, fighting the surging panic inside me.

"No, unfortunately there isn't," he said, adding that the good news—the *good news*! He actually said that!—was that I could make up the incompletes in summer school.

"But that means I won't graduate with my class!" I gasped. "Or walk across the stage and get my diploma!"

"Yes, I'm afraid that's true," he said sadly.

I couldn't *believe* it! You'd think they would have warned me! Or *reminded* me, at least!

"Well, can't you just let me get my diploma, then come back for summer school?" I asked.

"No, I'm very sorry, Tiffany. Those are the rules," he said. "We can't make an exception just for you."

"But I've already bought my dress for Grad Night!"

The room began to spin. Dean Schmitz kept talking, telling me that this was one of those painful but necessary learning experiences in the school of hard knocks, et cetera, et cetera, his words droning on like a swarm of bees.

I put my head between my knees, hyperventilating.

They say God never gives you more trouble than you can endure. But frankly, I think He's overestimating me.

I went back to class—what else could I do? Dropping out now would only make things worse, although how they could be *worse*, I could not imagine.

The news spread across the campus like wildfire. Campbell and The Girls rushed to my side, offering sympathy and support. Shelby suggested that I hire a lawyer. Even kids who've never liked me told me that they thought it wasn't fair, that I should at *least* get to walk across the stage and get my diploma.

"No," I said, "that wouldn't be right. They can't change the rules just for me."

But inside I was desperately screaming: *"WHY NOT??????????????"*

My parents were wonderful. They didn't get mad; they just looked really sad, which made me feel guilty. For years, they've dreamed of the moment when their little girl, all grown up now and ready to take on the world, would walk across the stage and collect her diploma. How happy and proud they would have been!

And I have robbed them of that joy.

That night, lying sleepless on my bed, I came to a deeper understanding of myself than I ever had before. I realized that I've been so wrapped up in my dreams of fame and fortune that I forgot to pay attention to real life—to all the little everyday details that make up the big picture.

There's more, much more to life than fame and glory. We all have to take out the trash sometimes, as a wise man once said.

But as I lay there in the dark, brimming with these newfound revelations, one question returned to haunt me, again and again:

Now what?

♥ ♥ ♥

It's odd, being at school, knowing that I'm not going to graduate with my friends. It's like I'm not a player anymore, but just a part of the audience.

People are being so nice to me. Too nice. You'd think I was in a *wheelchair* or something! I know they're thinking, *Poor Tiffany! She doesn't get to walk across the stage and collect her diploma or attend the Grad Night party.*

Graduation is only two weeks away. That's all people are talking about now. That, and what they plan to do this summer, and where they'll be going to college . . .

I know I brought this on myself, and that it's all my fault, so I shouldn't complain. But right now it feels like I'm standing all alone on the dock, watching my "friend-ships" sail away.

Miss Jones says I shouldn't let it get me down. "It's not the end of the world, Tiff," she said.

I know she means well, but she doesn't understand that it *is* the end of the world. *My* world. My high school years. The so-called happiest time of my life!

"Look at it this way, Tiff," she said. "This whole thing has been a valuable learning experience."

I think I'll start screaming if one more person says that!

"I know that," I said, "but it's just so disappointing! Besides, nobody's going to want to read my stupid book now, since I didn't turn out to be famous after all."

She started giving me that same old school-of-hard-knocks baloney, but I just put my head down on my desk and groaned.

"Miss Jones, you don't understand!" I moaned. "I wanted to be an *inspiration*!"

"Tiffany, dear," she said, gently patting my back. "Maybe you can still be an inspiration. Maybe you could—"

A lightbulb exploded in my brain. "Turn it into a self-help book?" I asked. "This happened to me; don't let it happen to you?"

"Well, perhaps," she said. "I wasn't thinking about a book. Something more along the lines of—"

"She who fails to prepare prepares to fail!" I exclaimed. "Exactly! Thank you, Miss Jones! Thank you! Thank you! I might even put your name in the dedication."

So even though I'm not famous—yet!—I can still help other young people like myself learn about stuff like life and love and rolling with the punches.

Which is all I ever really wanted anyway.

♥ ♥ ♥

The Girls have been wonderful. They're so supportive! But I don't know what I'd do without Campbell. I can tell him how I'm really feeling. Because believe me, it's not easy to put on a happy face and act like everything's just peachy while everybody's talking about graduation and the fun they'll have at the all-night party.

I feel so left out.

Campbell and I eat lunch together every day and most afternoons we drive up into the hills and just park the car and talk. I've never had a friend like Campbell before.

The other day he said, "I think you should appeal to the school board, Tiff. I don't see why they can't give you your diploma and let you complete your credits this summer."

"That's not the way it works," I explained, not mentioning that I'd tried that already. "I guess I'll just have to live with the consequences of my actions."

"But that doesn't seem fair," he said. He told me that he would get all of the kids to wear black armbands on their graduation gowns, in protest.

I gently but firmly told him no, that I didn't want to

disrupt the ceremony. The armbands wouldn't show up against the black gowns, anyway.

Still, it was a sweet gesture.

Everywhere I go, I see Mimi and Wally together. They make such a cute couple, with their matching tribal face scars, although Mimi's are just stenciled on, not permanent. Some of the kids started copying Wally, drawing on the spirals with marking pens. So now the school has passed a rule that nobody else can do it.

How could *anybody* fall for a dumb fad like that?

I ran into Mimi and Wally in the Senior Quad today. They were wrapped around each other like Siamese twins. Which I don't think is appropriate in public, but still, it's amazing how *right* they are for each other.

They told me that Mimi had been awarded a full scholarship to Stanford University, but that she's decided to turn it down. Instead, she and Wally are moving to Florida, where they'll attend Barnum & Bailey Clown College.

"It's just so obvious," Mimi explained, holding Wally's hand and smiling. "The world doesn't need another scientist."

"We feel that it needs more laughter," Wally finished.

I told them how happy I was for them, and by the time I was done, I realized that I actually meant it.

I'm so happy! Dean Schmitz just called and said I can go to the Grad Night party with Campbell, even though I'm not going to graduate!

Apparently, Campbell called all the school board members and bugged them until they said okay! This year's theme is "The S.S. *Hiram Johnson*," and the parents are making the gym look like a cruise ship. There'll be games and prizes and dancing—*all night!*—and at six o'clock in the morning they'll even serve us breakfast!

I can't *wait!*

My parents were thrilled when I told them I could go. But they looked worried when I said that I also plan to attend the ceremony so I can see my friends graduate.

"That will be too hard on you, Tiff," my father warned.

"Stay home with us until it's time for the party," my mother begged.

I told them that I've given the matter a lot of thought and have decided that I really want to be there in the audience for all of my friends, to honor and celebrate their moment of triumph.

"Don't worry," I assured my parents. "I'll be fine."

How could *anything* be worse than what I've been through already?

There was a big stinkola on campus today because the administration said that Mimi could *not* be the valedictorian after all, because it wouldn't look right, since her head is shaved.

The kids got so mad they practically went insane! We started a petition and got everyone to sign it, demanding that Mimi be allowed to give her speech or we wouldn't show up for the graduation ceremony. I mean, the people who are *in* the graduation ceremony.

Wally organized a walkout and the whole senior class left the building at 11 A.M., vowing to remain on the front lawn by the flagpole until the administration considered our demands.

I phoned the newspapers and the TV stations and they sent out reporters.

Talk about democracy in action! It was thrilling!

One of the Audiovisual Club guys whose name I can never remember gave Wally a portable microphone. He stood on the steps where everyone could see him and gave a speech. He said, "It's not important how people *look*. What matters is who they *are*." The crowd went wild and Principal Brown looked sick and Dean Schmitz told everyone to go inside and eat their lunches. But we wouldn't. Then two of the school board members drove up and I led the crowd in a cheer: "Give me an *M*! Give me an *I*! Now double it! What's that spell?" et cetera. The students roared and Mimi looked grateful; then the adults went inside to discuss the situation.

By the time they came back out, we were all getting pretty hungry, but it was worth it. Principal Brown announced that Mimi *can* be the valedictorian after all, as long as she keeps her mortarboard on her head!

The crowd clapped and cheered. Then a bunch of us went up and thanked Principal Brown and Dean Schmitz and the school board members, and shook their hands.

All in all, it was a very emotional and exciting morning!

But now the moment has come when I must put my maturity to the supreme test, and sit, all alone, in the audience, by myself, while my friends cross the stage to receive their diplomas, passing through the portal from childhood to adulthood.

On top of that, I've got cramps. Drat.

My parents wanted to accompany me to the graduation ceremony but I told them no, this was something I had to do alone. There were tears in their eyes as I left the house in my beautiful new pale-pink gown and matching shoes, my hair freshly trimmed and washed and tumbling down my back, brushed until it crackled with sparks.

But as I drove toward the campus, my heart started sinking, and I couldn't help thinking, Isn't it funny how things turn out? So different than you ever thought they would. I guess that's what makes life so interesting and suspenseful.

It's funny how things turn out.

People stared at me as I took my seat in the packed auditorium—not only because I was the only person in the audience wearing an evening gown, but because a lot of them knew who I was and why I wasn't sitting on the stage with my classmates.

I returned their pitying looks with brave smiles, but deep down inside, it really bugged me. It was like getting a bunch of condolence cards that read, "Too bad you forgot to graduate," or "Sorry you're such a dope."

Had coming to the ceremony been a terrible mistake? What if I jumped up and ran out crying when the choir began to sing "O Dolphins, Leap High"?

I couldn't, I simply *wouldn't*, let that happen. I was *not* going to spoil this evening for my friends—even if I had to put on the biggest act of my entire life!

"Dear God," I whispered, "give me strength. Thy Kingdom come, Thy Will be done, but *please* don't let me run out of here screaming, Amen."

I had a few bad moments when the ceremony started and The Girls—my Girls!—led the official school cheer without me. But I swallowed the lump in my throat and felt proud of them—it's not easy to do cartwheels in a graduation gown.

Then Janey Springer played the intro to "O Dolphins" on her oboe and the choir began to sing. And for one horrifying moment I thought I was losing control completely and was going to run out the door!

But God gave me strength and I gripped my chair so hard, I was afraid it would have to be *amputated* when the ceremony was over.

Then Ashley and Campbell—he never told me he had such a good voice . . . or maybe he did and I just don't remember—sang Little Tina's current hit, "We Are Your Children (So Get Used to It)," and the adults in the audience started crying. Ashley was so nervous she had to stand behind the curtain to sing, so all you could see were her shoes, but she used a mike and her voice carried beautifully.

Could Campbell see me in the crowd? Probably not, but I felt like he was singing just to me.

Then the speeches started and I realized something that I'd never known before: Graduation ceremonies can be very boring! Principal Brown just went on and on and *on*! Mostly, you couldn't understand what he was saying because the sound system was so crummy: "Honor *bzzddtt* integrity *bzzddtt* paths of life *bzzddtt* education," et cetera.

Finally it was time to hand out the awards for academic and athletic achievement.

As the school board members passed out the Certificates of Merit, I felt like I was going to *throw up*.

Tiffany, get a grip, I scolded myself. *You can't throw up NOW; people will think you're just jealous, and you'll ruin the ceremony for everybody else!*

Besides, I couldn't go to the Grad Night party with a bunch of stinky gook on my dress.

"And now," said Principal Brown, "I'm pleased to introduce this year's class valedictorian, Miss Mimi Durning. I'm sorry—*Ms*. Durning."

The audience buzzed when Mimi walked to the

podium. Her scalp was so slick the mortarboard kept slipping, and the spirals on her cheeks appeared freshly inked. But it turns out she's a really good speaker and the crowd fell silent when she started.

"I want to talk about frogs," Mimi said.

She said we have no business dissecting frogs or other animals because human beings are animals, too, and it's our God-given duty—I didn't know Mimi believed in God!—to respect and protect all living creatures. She said that we must act as responsible stewards for the planet so that our great-grandchildren and their great-grandchildren will honor us for not screwing things up any more than we possibly had to, et cetera.

"What does it profit a man or woman," Mimi asked, "if he/she gains the whole world but loses his/her soul?"

It was *stunning*. Even the kids tossing a beach ball around onstage stopped to listen. I felt so inspired by her speech I got goose bumps.

Finally she said, "I know that my classmates are anxious to receive their diplomas—"

"Party!" someone shouted.

"Thank you, Wally," she said, and the audience chuckled. "But before I conclude, I want to talk about school spirit. I used to think it was a joke. *Rah rah sis boom bah* and all that. But school spirit can be shown in many ways. For example . . ."

Suddenly, she whipped off her mortarboard and sailed it across the auditorium like a Frisbee. Painted on Mimi's gleaming scalp was some kind of ying/yang *amoeba* type of thing!

The audience gasped, and Dean Schmitz jumped up, looking like he wanted to *choke* her. Then everybody realized that the thing on Mimi's head was *two entwined dolphins* emblazoned in the school colors, black and red!

She waited until the cheering stopped before she continued.

"In closing," she said, "I would like to recognize someone whose energy, enthusiasm, and tremendous school spirit have played an enormous part on the stage of life and learning we call Hiram Johnson High. Please join me in giving a very special thank-you to Head Yell Leader, Tiffany Spratt. Stand up, Tiffany, so everyone can see you!"

My heart had stopped beating. My body was *frozen*. All around me, people clapped and called my name. *My name!*

The students onstage got to their feet—I couldn't *believe* it! They were leading the audience in a *standing ovation*!

I stood, my legs trembling. I was laughing and crying. Applause roared in my ears as I smiled and waved. But I didn't feel ashamed that everyone could see my tears. Instead, I felt so humble and so grateful.

Because in spite of everything, all my mistakes and flaws, and all of the little problems I'd caused, they were telling me, *Don't worry, Tiff, we love you,* with their hands.

I just wish I'd brought my video camera.